Secret Messages

BY

Henrietta F. Ford

Henrietta F. Ford

Enjoy!

Other Books by Henrietta F. Ford

Angels in the Snow

When Sleeping Dogs Lie

Murder on the OBX

The Hessian Link

The Grave House Guest

Galatia Road

Acknowledgements

In creating this novella, *Secret Messages,* I quickly realized how important it is to know people who are willing to share fresh ideas and their expertise. With this kind of support a simple story can quickly develop into a novel. I am fortunate enough to have such people in my book-writing world. For their help and encouragement I extend my deepest appreciation:

To Bonnie Enderly, an exceptional editor and dear friend…your superb skills made correcting and fine-tuning my work much simpler.

To Linda Eccleston, my friend and fellow author…your suggestions and willingness to provide "another pair of eyes" were most valuable.

To Lynn Bagley, English teacher extraordinaire…thank you for your eagle eye and questions that caused me to inquire more deeply.

To my husband, Jim Maus…without your input and support I could not have written this novella. Thank you for your encouragement and help.

Foreword

During the years between the Revolutionary War and Civil War thousands of slaves were helped to freedom via what would come to be known as the Underground Railroad. The Railroad was a moniker given northern routes that led to parts of the country that did not sanction slavery. It was hoped that upon arriving there the escaped slaves could live out their lives in freedom. There were guides... men and women, black and white...called "conductors" who knew these routes well and served over and over again as leaders over the treacherous trails. Theirs was a dangerous undertaking for to be caught aiding an escaped slave could result in a harsh and sometimes deadly judgment.

There were houses along the way that gave respite to weary slaves on their journey to freedom. These were called 'safe houses'. Such was the home of Dr. Charles Singletary, a physician in Seaboard, Northampton County, North Carolina. The Masonic symbol of square and compasses carved on the rock beside his backdoor indicated to conductors and run-away slaves that his home was a "safe house".

African slaves were accustomed to such symbols. In most parts of the African continent there was no alphabet; consequently, there was no written language. Pictographs were used to communicate. When slaves brought to America were skilled in working with textiles, wood carving and stone they used pictographs to communicate with each other. These secret messages took the form of carved symbols on wood and stone and pictures stitched into quilt patterns. They conveyed messages...messages hidden in plain view. And so it was that Bella, a free slave who worked for Dr. Singletary, possessed the skill of sewing pictographs onto quilts and linens. When a conductor was expected to arrive, Bella would hang a quilt containing symbols that announced his imminent arrival.

Characters

Dr. Charles Singletary—Seaboard doctor

Dr. Edward Singletary—Charles' Father

Dr. Robert Singletary—Charles' older brother

Dr. John Singletary— Charles' Grandfather and Singletary Patriarch

Dr. Rogers—Older Doctor, Dr. Charles Singletary's mentor

Mister Hathaway—Charles' travel host

Jerimiah—Hathaway's slave

Angela Singletary—Dr. Charles Singletary's wife

Millie (Mildred)—Dr. Singletary's oldest daughter

Lori (Dolores)—Dr. Singletary's second daughter

Willa (Wilhelmina)—Dr. Singletary's twin daughter

Willis—Dr. Singletary's twin son

Abel—Dr. Singletary's male servant

Bella—Dr. Singletary's woman servant and Abel's wife

Tiny—Bella's daughter

Sheriff Bland—Northampton County sheriff

Judge Madison—Friend of Dr. Singletary

Obadiah—escaped slave seeking refuge

Willis Too—Willa's child

PART I

The Decision

CHAPTER 1

The James River flowed intuitively, restlessly through the city of Richmond, Virginia on this warm autumn evening. The sky changed from blue to rosy to purple to gray until finally there was only an afterglow. Then an amazing golden harvest moon bounced from the horizon and glided majestically above the river. The water reflected small glittering specks of moonlight that looked like tiny silver coins sprinkled on the water.

The house that set above the river was a large structure built of bricks fired by slaves on the Singletary Plantation. The house, belonging to Dr. Edward Singletary, featured enormous white columns that lined the large porch, and chairs were arranged in small groups conducive to genteel conversation. In colonial time, plantations built on rivers certainly provided a stunning view; but the river also had a practical purpose. Rivers were natural highways. They provided transportation on which to move agricultural products to market. They also provided a way for the citizenry to travel, visit, and conduct business. In short, rivers were the lifeline of the communities.

That night music and laughter floated down from the grand house that overlooked the James. The music seemingly coaxed the river along its ancient course...a course that would ultimately end in the Atlantic Ocean. A path covered with crushed oyster shells led from the river to the house. It curved past English boxwoods and neatly tended flowerbeds. Century-old oaks and elms surrounded the garden providing shade from the hot Virginia summer sun. Deer often grazed on the lush lawn and songbirds and squirrels lived among the branches of the ancient trees.

Inside the house a celebration was taking place. Burnished floors made of heart pine sparkled. Fresh flowers adorned highly polished tables. Pewter and crystal chandeliers glowed in the radiance of candlelight and the smell of wax mingled with the scent of fine French perfume. The intricate molding and balusters on the curved staircase had been carved by an indentured servant who chose to work on the Singletary plantation long after his debt of passage was paid. On the wall along the stairwell, portraits of stern men and coy women smiled down at the goings-on below. Giggling young women flitted in and out of doors that opened onto the balcony above.

In the main hall, lovely ladies dressed in satin and lace flirted with young men from behind delicate fans woven with golden filigree. As their heads bobbed about in laughter, ostrich and peacock feathers pinned in their hair flounced about blithely. In the parlor, chairs and sofas rested against the walls providing seats for those who were not dancing. These seats were usually occupied by older gentry who enjoyed listening to the music provided by the musicians and remembering when they too glided across the dance floor with such grace and stamina.

Most eyes followed the guests of honor, Charles Singletary and his wife, Angela. Angela was noticeably with child and there were many whispers about the suitability of a woman in such condition exposing herself on the dance floor. But when Charles and Angela looked at each other so endearingly, no one could deny the love they felt for each other.

As Charles carefully led Angela across the dance floor he whispered, "How is our baby tonight?"

"Asleep, Charles," said Angela, "…safe and warm inside me."

Charles smiled and gently whirled her about. "Does it feel like a boy?"

Angela's face took on a serious expression and with some trepidation she said, "No, Charles. It doesn't. It feels like another girl. Would you be disappointed?"

Charles threw his head back and laughed,

"Disappointed? No! Now I shall have three lovely ladies to escort about." This time he whirled her less timidly and Angela squealed with delight.

Suddenly all eyes turned to the stairway and the room was filled with "Ahs"; "Isn't she adorable?"; "Precious". When Angela and Charles looked toward the stairs, their faces glowed with pride and love. Descending the stairs was a fully uniformed nurse, and she held tightly the hand of a small girl. The little girl was dressed in layers of soft white lace trimmed in blue satin. The long auburn curls that reached her shoulders were crowned with a large blue bow. She smiled brightly at the guests as she flounced down the steps. Angela Singletary's eyes filled with tears of joy, and Charles grinned brightly.

"Ah, here is my Mildred. Here is my beautiful little princess!" He rushed to the stairs, swooped up the child, and twirled her onto the dance floor. The musicians quickly understood the suggestion and broke into a lively ditty. Round and round Charles spun little Mildred as she shrieked with delight.

When the dance ended, Mildred raced to her mother and cried, "Mama, Mama, Papa danced me round and round!!!"

Angela bent over and embraced her daughter. "Yes Millie, Mama saw you and Daddy dancing, and what a beautiful pair you were!"

"I know. I know," giggled little Mildred. "We were the 'bestest' of all the dancers."

Everyone laughed. "Yes, my dear. You most certainly were the 'bestest' of them all," said Angela, and she hugged her little daughter again.

A bell tinkled from the hall entrance. Dr. Edward Singletary, Charles' father, faced his guests with authority. He was a tall, distinguished gentleman with silver-gray hair and a carefully trimmed beard. He held a glass of champagne high. "Honored guests, your attention please," he said in a voice that was obviously accustomed to being heard. "Tonight we are gathered to honor my second son, Charles, who has completed his medical studies and will soon join the ranks of other doctors in our family. Let us lift our glasses in congratulations to *Dr.* Charles Singletary. Everyone raised their glasses, drank a toast, and applauded.

"Speak! Speak!" the guests shouted.

Charles took Angela's hand and stepped forward. "Friends and colleagues thank you for joining Angela and me for this joyous celebration…and believe me it is a joy and a relief. There were times when I thought this night would never come." The guests laughed. "We have not yet…"

Suddenly, Dr. Edward Singletary interrupted. "Thank you, Charles, thank you. Now if the gentlemen would accompany me to the library for brandy and cigars…" And he abruptly turned, crossed the hall, and stepped toward the library.

A fire burned low in a fireplace made of river stones, and candlelight danced about the dark corners of the room. Paintings of horses, ships, and landscapes fitted into ornate frames adorned the oak-paneled walls. Stationed against a wall facing the fireplace was an enormous desk cluttered with envelopes, papers, and unopened correspondence. Another table stood against the opposite wall and a crystal decanter with matching brandy glasses set upon it. Servants in white coats and black pants poured brandy into the glasses, set them on silver trays, and moved among the guests dispensing the golden liquor. Cigars were passed in a similar manner, and soon smoke filled the air and voices became more jovial.

Dr. Charles Singletary moved among the men accepting their congratulations and listening as they shared accounts of their most interesting medical experiences. Charles enjoyed being among fellow doctors. The night was complete. Nothing could spoil the night when he was graciously accepted into the Richmond medical community.

Then suddenly, a boisterous voice erupted from the corner of the study. "Dr. Charles Singletary, tell us when you plan to join your father and brother in the

Singletary family practice?" All eyes turned to Charles.

Charles glanced quickly at his father. Dr. Edward Singletary smirked and looked down at the floor. Charles realized that the question being asked was not impromptu. His father had arranged for this guest to confront him with a decision that Dr. Edward Singletary had tried to force upon his son.

Charles turned toward the unruly guest and answered forthrightly. "Your question is one my father has asked me many times. But this is a decision that Angela and I have not yet made. When we make the decision, we shall announce it readily to our family and friends."

This seemed merely to energize the guest. "Why, surely there is no doubt you will join your father and brother in the family practice. Your father's practice would be incomplete without *both* sons on his staff. Have you had better offers?"

Charles became impatient with the prying guest.

He glared at his father to convey his awareness that the guest had been enlisted to question him publicly. Again, his father refused to meet his eye.

Charles stared at the guest and replied forcefully, "Practicing beside my brother and father would, of course, be an honor just as my father was honored to practice beside my grandfather. Yet, I am giving much thought to establishing my own practice in a place that is without a doctor…a place where the people are less fortunate, and I am truly needed… " Suddenly Charles was assaulted with a barrage of comments and questions.

"What…depart from your family calling?"

"If it is poor people you're looking for, you need not look farther than Richmond. We have plenty of poor people. You've just not looked in the right places."

"Sound decisions! At this point in your career, it's important to make sound decisions. Ask

19

yourself…"

And the yammer continued unabated. Suddenly a loud ***bang, bang*** sounded from the direction of the fireplace. All eyes turned toward a large wingback chair located there. Ensconced deeply in the winged-back chair was a small, wizened old man. The cane he held was almost as large as he, but he used it forcefully. ***Bam, bam, bam.*** Immediately, the voices were reduced to a mere murmur as all eyes fixed on the eldest Dr. Singletary…Dr. John Singletary. He was Charles' grandfather and the honored Singletary family patriarch. His fragile physical appearance did not reflect the voice that followed.

"I shall be heard!" his voice exploded. And his cane smacked the floor again emphatically. This time the room fell completely silent. "Tonight was to have been a joyous occasion for my grandson, Charles. Instead it has been reduced to an inquisition. Your questions have diminished his accomplishments. You have intruded upon what should have been ***his*** happiest moment and ***my*** proudest. This is greatly resented."

Guests lowered their heads in embarrassment and the old gentlemen continued, "My grandson, Charles, possesses a spirit of adventure and a passion to heal the sick that have no medical care. This family has practiced medicine for three generations, and I have waited for signs of such selflessness in my progeny. Finally, I witness the kind of self-sacrifice that all men of healing should possess. This family has received much in my lifetime, and wherever Charles' decision takes him, he will take with him his full portion of the family fortune. It is time to give back. To my grandson, Dr. Charles Singletary, I say, cheers!" And the old gentleman nodded to Charles, lifted his glass, and drank.

The guests, Dr. Edward Singletary, and Brother Robert echoed the salute. "Cheers! Cheers! Cheers!"

"Now, shall we join the ladies?" said Grandfather Singletary. He positioned himself to stand.

Charles rushed forward and took his arm. As Grandfather stood, Charles said, "Thank you,

Grandfather. I shall try to not let you down."

The wise old man paused, looked at his grandson, and said, "It is not *I* you should hope not to disappoint but yourself. Remember, '...to *oneself* be true'. Charles, I honor your decision; and furthermore, I shall support your mission by subsidizing your clinic. Therefore it is up to you, Charles, to complete this undertaking." Grandfather smiled reassuringly at Charles then shuffled slowly toward the door.

Charles stood alone in the library. He acknowledged that his motives for establishing his own practice were not entirely altruistic. Charles' father planned to bequeath his estate according to the old English tradition which dictated that the oldest son inherit everything. Charles, being the younger son, was to be left to his own devices. He was confident Robert would welcome him into the family practice, but ownership of the practice, the plantation, and all of Dr. Edward Singletary's possessions would be inherited by Robert.

The music began, and as he stepped toward the door, he heard soft applause. Then a stranger stepped silently from behind the bookcase. At first Charles was startled, but the stranger's engaging smile was reassuring. He looked to be about the age of Charles' father. He was not as elegantly dressed as the other guests. His haircut was ragged and his beard looked to have been trimmed by an untrained hand. His tan skin hinted at hours in the summer sun, and his hands were rough and red. Yet, he had an air about him that exuded confidence and strength.

"Excuse me, Dr. Charles Singletary. I am Dr. Rogers. Your father and I attended medical school at the same time. I want to personally congratulate you."

"Thank you, Dr. Rogers," Charles said with some trepidation.

"I also want to ask if you are sincere about establishing a practice fixed simply on the needs of the less fortunate."

Charles feared that Dr. Rogers was among those selected by his father to pressure him into joining his family practice. Then he remembered his grandfather's words and summoned the confidence to reply forcefully, "Yes Dr. Rogers, I am most serious about establishing a practice that will serve those less fortunate. And I don't want to do it in Richmond. In Richmond, the temptation to rely on my family would be too great. I want my work to be *my* mission, and my mission is to help those who most need help." Charles turned toward the door.

"I admire your determination, Charles," said Dr. Rogers. "Now I want to extend an invitation...an invitation to accompany me to a place that might fit your purposes. Come. See for yourself what it would be like to live and practice medicine in a place where there are so many less fortunate. You will find that this place has many poor, needy, and disenfranchised who desperately need medical care."

Charles' interest was suddenly peaked. He turned to the old doctor. "Where is this place?"

"It is a small village in eastern Carolina. Concord. It is but a two day ride by horse."

Charles stepped closer. Now he was definitely interested. "Is this where you live, Doctor?" asked Charles.

"No. I live in yet another village seven miles away. Jackson. For many years I have struggled to serve both towns, but now I am getting too old. Too tired. A young, strong doctor like you would go a long way to lightening my load. Come see for yourself.

"Concord is a needy community and you must not think that you will always be paid money for your services. But what you fail to receive in money, you will get back tenfold in love and appreciation…and maybe chickens." Dr. Rogers laughed and moved closer to Charles. "One morning I awakened to find ten chickens on my back porch as payment for my services. I wondered how ten chickens possibly covered my entire bill. But that winter I had eggs to eat, and in the spring I counted twenty baby chicks scratching along behind the mother hens." Both men laughed.

How bucolic and peaceful Concord sounded to Charles. He said, "Dr. Rogers, I would very much like to visit the village of Concord. When shall we leave?"

CHAPTER 2

An enormous orange ball bounced above the giant magnolia and pecan trees. Charles and Angela stood ankle deep in a fine mist that hovered just above the ground. A servant stood nearby holding the reins of a handsome white horse while Little Mildred fed it carrots. Charles drew Angela to him and tenderly caressed her belly.

"Take care of our baby," he whispered, and gently brushed a kiss across her cheek.

"Oh I shall, Charles. I shall take good care of her," Angela whispered. "She will be safe inside me until you return to celebrate her birth."

They heard the distant sound of approaching hoofs. Soon Dr. Rogers appeared through the fog. He tipped his hat, bowed, and said, "Good morning to you, Dr.

and Mrs. Singletary." Then he saw Little Mildred and added, "…and to you too, little lady."

Dr. Rogers' horse became restless and he said, "Shall we go, Charles? We have quite a ride ahead of us today. I promised a friend that we would accept his hospitality this evening, and he will have a feast prepared for us at sundown."

"Certainly," said Charles and he turned to Angela and embraced her one last time.

Mildred squealed and raced to Charles. "Me too, daddy. Kiss Millie bye."

Charles swept Millie up into his arms. "I shan't be gone long, Millie, and I shall bring you a surprise when I return." Charles kissed his daughter, turned her toward Angela, and said, "Go now."

The men turned their horses south and galloped away. From an upstairs window of the big house, two men looked down at the scene below. As the two doctors rode away, Dr. Edward Singletary casted his eyes downward and slowly shook his head while Brother Robert's face took on a faint smile.

&&&

At first, Charles recognized some of the farmsteads and manor houses along the way. But soon the city of Richmond was behind them and the horses slowed to a peaceful trot. Now in unfamiliar surroundings, Charles thought the countryside to be quiet, rustic, pastoral.

Beautiful horses grazed in fields behind rail fences. A young stallion reared his head and, sensing a race was afoot, trotted along the fencerow keeping pace with the men's horses. Another young horse joined in the competition until, finally, the men disappeared down the dusty road and the fenced horses returned to grazing.

Acres of tobacco fields skirted the road with their yellow leaves ripe for pulling. Black men and women stripped the leaves from the stalks and tossed them onto a wooden sled. The sled was pulled by a stubborn mule that was being coaxed by a young boy. Charles was surprised to see such young children working in the fields. The sled boy was coated with dust, making it difficult to attest to the true hue of his skin. Beyond the tobacco field was a large barn. Inside, he could see workers lift the tobacco leaves off the sled, tie the leaves into bunches, and hang them to dry on long wooden poles that extended from one side of the barn loft to the other.

The fields beyond looked quite different. Here, the ground appeared to be covered with snow. Boles of cotton hung heavily from the plants, and black women and young girls moved methodically through the field picking the cotton and putting it into large cloth sacks. Charles spotted a very young child sleeping soundly under a shade tree atop one of the sacks filled with soft cotton. Nearby, the child's watchful mother continued to drag her sack down the rows, pick cotton, and put the cotton in the sack.

The sun reached its zenith, and workers slowly left

the fields and found shade under nearby trees. Once they were settled, kitchen slaves passed metal plates of food to the workers. Charles could not see what was on the plate but he was reminded that many hours had passed since he'd breakfasted.

Apparently Dr. Rogers felt hungry too. "Just ahead is a stream," said Dr. Rogers. "It's a suitable place to take our noonday meal." Charles nodded in agreement and they spurred the horses on.

They soon reached a stand of trees. A clearing had been created by previous travelers who also found the spot to be inviting. They dropped the horses' reins, thus allowing them to wade into the cool, shallow stream. Then the men sought privacy in order to relieve their own discomfort. Charles opened the leather nap-sack containing their lunch of dried meat jerky, bread, cheese, and apples. They ate slowly, savoring the meal and enjoying the tranquility of the surroundings. The trees were alive with birds and squirrels. A buck edged its way toward the stream, saw the travelers, and retreated quickly. The men chuckled.

After taking the noon sustenance, the men fell into relaxed conversation. Dr. Rogers told Charles about Concord. He spoke of the poor farmers that worked the land that surrounded the village. He also spoke of the more affluent land owners. Dr. Rogers hastened to add that affluent land owners in the Northampton County area did not compare in wealth to Richmond gentry. He spoke of the village of Concord in Northampton County with its small houses, well-kept flower beds, and kitchen gardens. He described nearby churches and explained that efforts were being made to locate churches within the village of Concord itself. Dr. Rogers knew Charles was a Mason and so he told him where Masonic Lodges were located. He even shared a rumor he'd heard that a railroad might be built to run through Concord on its route to Portsmouth, Virginia.

Dr. Rogers reminded Charles again that he would have many patients, but he should not expect to become a wealthy doctor like the doctor members of his family. He quickly added, however, that Charles' services would make him a much loved and appreciated physician. It was during this amiable conversation that Charles revealed his aversion to slavery and how pained he felt to see the black slaves working the fields from dawn to sunset with little to eat and no recompense.

Dr. Rogers nodded and his face took on a look of empathy. Then he abruptly stood, stretched, and said, "Now we should travel on if we are to arrive at the home of our host on time. He is expecting us for dinner at sundown. His name is Hathaway. He is a widower and lives alone. He welcomes company and night guests. Tomorrow we shall begin our ride early, and arrive shortly in Carolina," said Dr. Rogers.

Chapter 3

Charles and Dr. Rogers reached the lane that led to their host's manor house just as the sun dipped toward the western horizon. As they rode toward the house, they passed slaves looking weary and covered with dust. They slowly plodded their way toward the cabins that sat behind the manor house. Large iron pots stood among the cabins, and a delicious aroma wafted into the air as women prepared the slaves' evening meal.

As they arrived at the house, a well-dressed gentleman stepped upon the porch and beckoned to the riders. "Welcome. You must be very tired and hungry. Welcome to my home."

Charles and Dr. Rogers dismounted, removed their hats and bowed to their host. "Thank you for your hospitality, my friend. Yes, we are tired and we are hungry. But I must say that ours was a pleasant trip.

May I introduce my traveling companion, Dr. Charles Singletary? Charles, this is our gracious host, Mr. Austin Hathaway."

The two men shook hands, and then Hathaway led them into the house and into the library. "Let us have a glass of sherry while the meal is being laid on the table. Then we shall eat and you can tell me all about your trip and your purpose for such."

The glass of the sherry served the travelers well. It not only warmed them, but it loosened their tongues. When their meal was laid before them, dinner conversation flowed freely as Charles explained his intentions to provide medical care to anyone needing it … especially the poor. Dr. Rogers then explained that his purpose on the trip was to accompany Charles to just such a place…Concord, over in North Carolina.

"Ah Charles, what a worthy challenge! In Concord you will doubtless find many who need medical attention. And you will most certainly find many who are poor. I salute you." And he lifted his glass to Charles.

Spirits were high and Charles and Dr. Rogers found their host to be most gracious as well as entertaining. "I say, gentlemen," Hathaway said, "Have you ever seen a slave read?" Charles and Dr. Rogers replied that they had not. "Well, see here, you shall see one do just that tonight. He turned to the waiting servant who stood silently in the corner of the dining room and said, "Fetch Jerimiah for me."

The waiting servant scurried from the room and returned quickly accompanied by a young mulatto boy who looked to be about sixteen. He was dressed much better than the other slaves the doctors had seen and, unlike the other slaves, he carried himself with confidence.

"Jerimiah, fetch my Bible from that shelf," Mr. Hathaway said. The boy immediately went to the shelf, fetched the Bible, and handed it to Mr. Hathaway who refused to take it. He nodded to Charles. "No, give it to Dr. Singletary." The boy complied.

Then Hathaway turned to Charles. "Find a passage…any passage and give it back to Jerimiah."

Charles didn't want the boy to be fooled, but he followed Mr. Hathaway instructions and turned to a chapter in the book of Ecclesiastes. Then, with some trepidation, Charles handed the Bible back to Jerimiah and said, "Jerimiah this is my favorite reading."

"Now," continued Mr. Hathaway, "Jerimiah, read the passage Dr. Singletary selected aloud."

Jerimiah did not seem the least nonplused. He held the Bible proudly and began to read, *"To everything there is a season, and a time to every purpose under the heaven, A time to be born and a time to die, a time to ………"*

When Jerimiah finished, Dr. Rogers said, "I was under the impression that it was forbidden to …"

Mr. Hathaway cut him short and banged his fist on the table. "Jerimiah is my property. I shall do what I want with him and teach him what I like."

Charles and Dr. Rogers were taken aback by Hathaway's sudden outburst which led them to believe that he had been previously questioned about teaching a slave to read. Then their host looked embarrassed. He said, "Forgive me gentlemen. Jerimiah, give Dr. Rogers the Bible." Jerimiah complied. "Dr. Rogers, select any psalm…any psalm at all. Go ahead. Pick a Psalm."

Dr. Rogers opened the Bible and nodded. "I have done so," he said. Fearing that Jerimiah would not be familiar with all the psalms, he chose one of the most well-known, "I choose the twenty-third psalm."

"Oh that is too easy, isn't it, Jerimiah," Mr. Hathaway chuckled. "But go ahead. Recite the twenty third psalm."

Without any hesitation Jerimiah began to recite, *"The Lord is my shepherd; I shall not want. He maketh me to lie down in green pastures: He leadeth me beside the still waters…."*

When Jerimiah completed his recitation, Hathaway laughed so hard tears ran down his face. Jerimiah looked proudly at the guests.

Charles wondered how Mr. Hathaway would have reacted if Jerimiah had not been able to read Ecclesiastes or if he had made a mistake in the recitation of the twenty-third psalm.

"Now Jerimiah, show the gentlemen how you know arithmetic. If Dr. Singletary had twelve chickens," and he pointed his fork at Charles. "And Dr. Rogers had fifteen chickens, how many chickens would they have all together?"

Jerimiah didn't hesitate, "Twenty-seven," he said.

Charles and Dr. Rogers started to congratulate Jerimiah and Hathaway said, "No. Wait, wait. Now Jerimiah, if a weasel got into the chicken house and ate four chickens, how many would the doctors have left?"

"Twenty- three," Jerimiah quickly answered.

Mr. Hathaway laughed. "It's not a trick. Jerimiah can do numbers. Thank you, Jerimiah. You may go now."

After dinner, the men returned to the library where brandy was generously served and conversation continued way into the night. Finally, Dr. Rogers declared that he must have sleep if they were to reach Concord the next day. Charles and Dr. Rogers thanked their host effusively for his hospitality, bid him goodnight, and wearily headed toward the stairs. As they climbed the stairs, Charles glanced into the kitchen. There he saw Jerimiah huddled in the corner. He held a book tilted toward the light. His lips moved silently as his fingers slowly touched each word on the page. Charles was still taken aback, he knew it was unlawful to teach slaves to read.

Chapter 4

It was another warm Indian summer morning. The sun shone through the red and orange leaves. A gentle breeze stirred the trees causing a cascade of golden leaves to float like golden coins to the ground. Drs. Rogers and Singletary awoke early, splashed cold water from the basin on their faces, and hurried downstairs. There, a breakfast feast was laid for them. Hathaway, however, was not present. They learned that he was needed in the birthing of a calf. Anxious as they were to continue their journey, they ate heartily and spoke little.

As the doctors stepped onto the porch, their host appeared from the direction of the barn. "Ha," said Dr. Rogers. "I suppose all went well with the birthing since you did not call on either of us for assistance."

Mr. Hathaway chuckled. "Yes, all went well. Although I did not require a physician's assistance, it was reassuring to know medical help was nearby. Safe journey, gentlemen," he said and extended his hand to each man. "Now Dr. Singletary, I shall be anxious to learn if Concord is the place you are looking for."

& & &

Charles and Dr. Rogers rode south toward the Virginia-North Carolina boundary. Dr. Rogers apprised Charles of the early history of this village that might become his home. Charles learned that the village had approximately 500 people. It was built in 1751 by settlers from Virginia who were attracted to the fertile farm land. They called their village Concord, and Concord became a thoroughfare between the Roanoke River and larger towns of Virginia.

Being an avid churchgoer, Dr. Rogers related how churches were an important part in the early lives of the settlers of Concord. Even though there were no churches in the village of Concord, villagers attended various churches in Northampton County. Visiting preachers often frequented this part of Carolina.

Dr. Rogers suggested the Methodist Meeting House about four miles from Concord, which had been built in 1795. It was simply called the Concord Meeting House. Although the one-room building was small, it possessed many features of which the congregation was proud. Front entry into the building was through double doors, and three clear glass windows were on each side of the House. The timbers underneath were hand-hewn and the bricks handmade. Inside the Meeting House the ceilings were batten-board, the floors cut pine, and the pews and railings were handmade. All this work was faithfully done by men of the Methodist Meeting House.

Dr. Rogers did not want Charles to think that Concord would always be without its own church. He hastily assured Charles that the proud and devoutly religious citizens of Concord were anxious to build a house of worship there in the village of Concord. It appeared that their spirit was high but their pockets were empty.

Charles listened with real interest as Dr. Rogers told how the citizens of the small village had a real concern for education. Parents encouraged their young children to learn their ABC's, study their numbers, and read Bible stories, such as the ones told them at the country churches. As father of two young children, Charles was pleased to learn there was a former school teacher in Concord who taught reading, writing, and arithmetic in her home.

As they approached a fork in the road, the dusty road soon turned to mud. Trees reached out of a murky green swamp and they were assaulted by the smell of mold and rot. The horses were thirsty after such a long dusty ride and wanted to drink from the marsh, but Dr. Rogers and Charles steered them away from the shallow, slimy ponds.

"There's fresh water just ahead," Dr. Rogers pointed and added, "Concord's just up that hill." And he urged his mount forward. Charles followed.

When they reached the summit of the hill, the two riders paused and Charles looked down upon the place that could become his home. They approached slowly as Charles thoughtfully studied the village from a distance. This was the time he would make life-changing decisions for himself and his family. Could he establish a medical practice in a place like this? Could Angela endure the harshness that would come with life in this backwoods location? Could his children survive in a wilderness like the one they had just traveled through?

Dr. Rogers studied Charles' face. He wondered what Charles was thinking about the place in which he now found himself. He wondered if any of the stories he'd shared over the last two days could possibly influence Charles to bring the medical help that Concord so badly needed. Dr. Rogers had tried to be brutally honest. Was he perhaps too honest? Dr. Rogers became increasingly nervous as he looked for some indication of Charles' feelings. How he wished he could read Charles' mind.

As they rode closer to the town, Charles noted the first houses on the farrowed, muddy road. They were small one-story plank dwellings. A few were white-washed but most were unpainted. Poorly dressed, barefoot children played in the yards and splashed in the mud puddles. Chickens roamed freely in the yards and a one-eared cat groomed itself in a sunny spot of a porch. A woman was spreading laundry on tree limbs and bushes to dry. She stopped and stared at the stranger riding beside Dr. Rogers. Two cur dogs spotted the riders, barked, and fell in behind their horses.

As the men proceeded closer to town, Charles realized that the citizens' circumstances here seemed better than he had expected. Here, the houses were painted and there were several two-story homes. Porches and yards were swept and an occasional flower bed retained remnants of its summer bloom. Clean, well-dressed children raced about the yard under the watchful eye of a black nannie. In a kitchen garden, an almond-colored male slave gathered root vegetables.

Charles noticed several cabins in back of the houses and recognized them to be slave cabins. Notwithstanding, the slave cabins were painted white. A lady opened the front door, shielded her eyes from the bright morning sun, and stared at the two horsemen.

Dr. Rogers tipped his hat, nodded his head, and said, "Good morning to you Mrs. Adams. Fine day, isn't it?"

"Why Dr. Rogers, I didn't recognize you," she replied as she continued to stare.

Several houses were similar to Mrs. Adams' home in style. As they continued toward the center of town, they passed one house on which construction seemed to have been halted. The place stood empty and no one was there to complete the construction. Dr. Rogers noticed Charles staring at the house. "Mr. Floyd Cramer started building that house for his wife. She died in February. He died in March. I've noticed this often in elderly patients...when one spouse dies the other soon follows." Then Dr. Rogers added dismissively, "Nonetheless, that house would have been too large for them anyway."

As they reached the bottom of the hill, Charles asked, "Where are the slaves? There are several slave cabins behind the Adams' place but only two slaves."

"Off to the fields outside of town," said Dr. Rogers and he brought his horse to a standstill in front of a group of six men. "Well here we are, Dr. Singletary. You have officially arrived in the *center of Concord*."

Charles studied the *center of Concord*. There was a general merchandise store with bins of root vegetables and greens brought in from the nearby gardens. Bolts of yard goods were strewn on roughly hewn tables and a large basket was filled with new and used children's shoes. A glass jar of tempting hard candy was set near the basket of shoes. A leg of smoked ham hung above a cutting board and loaves of freshly baked bread set in a large basket on a nearby table. Charles noticed the ham and bread were covered with flies. Sundry items gathered dust on shelves and tables, and in the center of the room there was an iron stove surrounded by wooden chairs.

Across the road from the general merchandise store was a wheelwright shop. Wheel rims, wooden spokes, and metal wheels hung from the walls of the shop. Several wooden carts awaited repair as the wheelwright struggled to complete repairs on a baby buggy. The wheelwright stopped his work and eyed the stranger with Dr. Rogers. When he noticed men gathering across the road, he laid down his awl and hurried to join them.

Dr. Rogers and Charles dismounted and joined the men. Dr. Rogers spoke authoritatively, "Gentlemen, may I introduce my friend and colleague, Dr. Charles Singletary, from up Richmond, Virginia. Dr. Singletary is looking for a suitable place to establish his medical practice and I am hoping that he will consider Concord. Should Dr. Singletary choose to open a practice here, Concord will have a full-time doctor, and my workload will lessen in my waning years." Now Dr. Rogers had the complete attention of the men. At that point he briefly presented Dr. Charles Singletary's resume. The men listened closely as he spoke and Dr. Rogers was pleased to see many nods of approval. When he finished his presentation Dr. Rogers moved through the small crowd and introduced Charles to each man.

For much of the afternoon Charles' new acquaintances inundated him with stories about life in Concord. The group attracted an even larger crowd and it seemed that everyone had something to tell. Charles often found it difficult to follow conversations as everyone talked at once. They told him how farmers from Virginia were attracted to the fertile farm land and chose to migrate. They spoke with pride of how they established Concord and predicted the little village would most certainly grow and prosper. Charles had already been told much of what they said, but he enjoyed their enthusiasm and listened intently.

Finally Charles said, "Gentlemen, you have told me much to help me make my decision. I understand there is a need for medical help in Concord, and I am most anxious to provide that help. Therefore, Concord will be my new home."

There was much handshaking and backslapping as the young doctor struggled to remember the names of his new neighbors. Dr. Rogers stood aside, smiled broadly, and relaxed.

Charles raised a palm up and everyone fell silent. He said, "Now, perhaps you can help me. I must move my family to Concord as soon as possible, and I have no place in which to move them." There was muttering among the men. Charles spoke again. "I noticed a partially built house a short distance back and it appears to be a house that would suit my family. I need to know the name of the builder. Perhaps he would finish the house to serve as my home and office. Could someone give me the name of this builder?"

Again everyone spoke at once, but one voice out-shouted the others. The man stepped forward. *"I shall give him his name.* The builder is my father. Doctor, I shall introduce you to him."

"Thank you, sir," said Charles. "If convenient, I would like to meet him this afternoon at the house." The man simply nodded, turned, and walked away. Everyone was reluctant to end the public gathering, so Charles moved unhurriedly through the crowd. There were more handshakes and backslapping. Charles modestly acknowledged their appreciation for establishing his practice in Concord, and they wished him a safe move from Richmond to Concord.

As Dr. Rogers and Charles rode up the hill toward the house, Dr. Rogers searched Charles face for signs of doubt. He said, "That was a swift decision you made back there, Dr. Singletary."

Charles looked anxious. "I hope I made the right one."

"Important decisions must often be made quickly," Dr. Rogers counseled.

Charles planned to use the money Grandfather Singletary gave him for completion of the house and the addition of an office. He would name the office after his benefactor. It would be called the Dr. John Singletary Clinic.

They arrived at the site of the unfinished house. Two men stood under a large elm tree. The younger stepped toward Charles. Now, he was uneasy and spoke softly. "Dr. Singletary, I must tell you my father can neither read nor write, but if you walk him through the house and tell him exactly what you want done, he will remember and carry out your instructions without error."

At first Charles was incredulous. How could he return to Richmond and leave the building of his home and office to an illiterate builder? Then he heard Dr. Rogers clear his throat. Charles turned to see Dr. Rogers splay his hands and shrug his shoulders. Suddenly, Charles realized expectations in Concord were quite different from those in Richmond.

Charles walked to the man standing under the tree and held out his hand. The old man shook his hand nervously.   Then Charles placed his arm on the builder's shoulder and said, "Mr. Davis, I am Dr. Singletary. Let's step inside. If you can gather enough workers, I need you to build me a house with an attached office."

Chapter 5

Charles was awakened by the sound of a cock crowing. He slipped out of the warm bed, padded across the cold floor, and looked out the window. The sun was breeching the horizon and the sky was a rosy hue. The smell of sizzling bacon wafted through the house and Charles couldn't remember the last time he'd eaten. Charles attended to his morning needs, quickly put on his clothes, and followed the delicious scent down the stairs and to the kitchen.

As he walked into the room he was greeted with a cheery, "Good morning to you, Doctor Singletary."

"Good morning to you, Mrs. Rogers. Something smells good," replied Charles.

"Yes, and you'll be wantin' a nice cuppa tea now won't you...or would you rather have coffee?" she said.

Mrs. Rogers was a plump woman with a round rosy face set with sparkling blue eyes. She wore a cotton print dress and her hair was drawn up in a severe white bun on the top of her head. She had a smile that lit up the morning and spoke with a distinct Irish accent. Her family was Irish immigrants who immigrated to this country, and she proudly held on to their manner of speech and their style of cooking.

"Coffee would be nice please, Mrs. Rogers. That might serve me better on my ride," said Charles.

Mrs. Rogers placed a mug in front of Charles and poured him a large cup of thick black brew. "Now," she said, "I have packed you a small lunch of dried meat and sour dough bread. It's not much but it'll hold you on your journey."

"Thank you, Mrs. Rogers, for your graciousness and hospitality," said Charles.

"Oh, be done with ye, Doctor, it's the least I can do for someone who's going to lighten my husband's load. Ye were sent by God, Dr. Charles Singletary. I have prayed and prayed for someone to come who would take some of the burden from the shoulders of Dr. Rogers...and you were most certainly sent in answer to my prayers."

"So...you've been praying over me again have you, woman?" said Dr. Rogers as he entered the kitchen. "I always say be careful what you pray for...your prayer might be answered."

Mrs. Rogers laughed cheerfully. "Well, they were certainly answered this time." And she lifted her face upward, closed her eyes, and said, "I thank the dear Lord."

Doctor Rogers eyed his wife lovingly. Charles looked away shyly as he glimpsed an affectionate look pass between them.

Charles ate hurriedly. "I'm most anxious to get started," he said.

"Your horse is waiting for you already. Will you stay at Hathaway's this evening?" asked Dr. Rogers.

"Yes. That is a half-way point of the trip and I look forward to telling him of my opinions and decision."

Charles pushed away from the table, thanked Mrs. Rogers again for her hospitality, and hurried outside. There was a nip in the air...the promise of winter to come. A servant held the reins of his saddled horse. The horse was impatient and stomped about puffing great clouds of white condensation into the morning air. Charles pulled himself up into the saddle, waved to Dr. and Mrs. Rogers and turned his horse north.

Charles did not make his ride home as leisurely as the previous trip. He was anxious to reach his next waypoint, Mr. Hathaway's place. Charles realized that even his horse seemed impatient. Charles stopped at the spot where he and Dr. Rogers had eaten their lunch. He released his horse's reins and the horse went immediately into the cold stream. Charles found the dried meat and sourdough biscuits to be delicious, and was surprised at how hungry he was after such a large breakfast.

After coaxing his horse from the stream, Charles saddled up and rode in the direction of the Hathaway place. He hoped to arrive before suppertime. Again, he passed slaves wearily trudging toward the cabins behind the big manor house.

When he arrived at the house he was surprised to see the wait servant standing on the porch to greet him.

"Welcome, Dr. Singletary," said the servant. "Mastuh Hathaway ain't here. He gone to Williamsburg and is sorry he missed you. But he says to tell you welcome, and that dinner and your bed are ready."

"That is very gracious of him. I'm sorry I missed him," said Charles as he handed the reins of his horse to a yard servant.

Charles passed through the door and headed toward the staircase. "I would like to wash up in my room," and he quickly ascended the steps. He found that the room he'd shared with Dr. Rogers was already prepared for him. He splashed cold water on his face and neck and stretched out on the bed to rest. Today, the miles had slipped by quickly and, with each mile, he felt Angela's presence grow stronger. After a short respite, he woke up abruptly. At first he did not know where he was. Slowly, awareness returned and he sat up with a start. He missed Angela yet he felt her closeness so strongly. He reminded himself that tomorrow he would be with his lovely wife.

The wait servant heard Charles moving about in his room. He immediately laid out a lavish meal on the big dining table and set a single lonely place. When Charles came downstairs he went directly to the dining room. His meager lunch had failed to sustain him long ago, so he ravenously ate of the feast before him. The servant who had greeted him upon his arrival stood aside for Charles' service. It occurred to Charles that he had not seen the young mulatto who read so eloquently for Dr. Rogers and him on his last visit.

Charles turned to the wait servant, "Where is the young boy who read for Dr. Rogers and me on my last visit?" he asked.

"He went to Williamsburg with Mastuh Hathaway," the servant said.

The meal was delicious. There were several fall root vegetables, a fresh pork roast, a fine home-blend muscatel wine, and fresh apple dumplings for dessert. The servant continuously refilled Charles' wine glass and by the end of the meal Charles felt replete, exhausted, and a little drunk.

Charles placed his napkin on the table and started to stand. The wait servant rushed to hold his chair. Charles walked unsteadily to the stairway and started up the steps. Suddenly he stopped and glanced into the kitchen at the corner where he'd seen the boy intensely studying a book. Charles wondered at the strange relationship between the mulatto boy and Mr. Hathaway.

Chapter 6

Miles passed and the terrain became more familiar to Charles. He recognized the farms and beautiful manor houses. Their owners often visited the Singletary home for business purposes, parties and celebrations. He rode along the James River for several miles and recalled the many adventures he had as a child on the water and muddy banks. He watched barges move slowly up and down the river carrying supplies or merchandise to docks. He wondered if he would ever see these scenes again after he moved to North Carolina. Would he miss the place he'd lived all his life? The closer he came to his Richmond home, the swifter his horse moved.

As doubts flooded his mind Charles spurred his horse on faster toward Richmond proper, toward home, and toward Angela. He wondered if he would lose the bond with his family. Would he grow to regret the decision to reject his father's wish for him to join the family practice in Richmond? Was it reckless to move

Millie from Richmond to a little town that could not possibly offer the amenities of a large city? Could Angela who grew up in society with servants, social events, and finery adjust to a backwoods environment such as Concord?

Finally, the sight of his home in the distance forced him to push negative thoughts from his mind. He did not need to urge his horse onward. The horse recognized the surroundings and knew that when they reached that place in the distance, a trough of oats awaited him.

When Charles arrived at the house he swung from the saddle even before the horse completely stopped. A servant ran to the horse, caught the reins, and said, "Welcome home Dr. Charles,"

"Thank you, Isaac," Charles called as he hurried up the steps to the front door. He flung the door open and stepped into the hall, startling a woman who was scrubbing the floor.

"Why, Dr. Charles," she said, "You 'bout scared the wits outta me."

"Where is Angela?" Charles said.

"Why she's..." the woman answered as Charles rushed up the steps.

As Charles reached the landing he saw a nurse leaving Angela's room. "Why are you here? Is Angela alright?" he asked as he continued to move toward her door.

"Why, Dr. Charles," said the nurse with a big grin on her face, "Mrs. Angela is just fine and so is your new baby."

Charles stopped abruptly. "My new baby?" he asked incredulously.

"Why, yes sir, a fine little girl," she said.

Charles opened the door to his wife's room and there propped against a mountain of pillows, was his smiling Angel…Angela. He also spied a little head of red curls leaning over a wooden cradle.

"Angela," Charles said, "Are you okay?" She held her hands out to him. He rushed to her side, held her close, and kissed her soft hair.

"Charles, Charles," Angela said. "I am just fine and so is your new daughter." She gestured toward the crib where Millie held her sister's tiny finger.

"Papa, Papa, look, we have a baby…a brand new baby. Her name is colora…loris…her name is…"

Charles and Angela smiled. "I have named her Dolores as we agreed," said Angela. "Millie is just having a bit of trouble with the pronunciation."

Charles reached into the crib and gently lifted the tiny baby. Her little head barely filled his hand. She squirmed and her rosebud mouth reached toward Charles' shirt.

"Her want to nurse," said Millie. "Her think you

Mama." Charles and Angela smiled.

"Angela, she is so small," said Charles. "And she is early. Are you sure she's well?"

Angela said, "She nurses vigorously, sleeps well, and is quite alert. She is fine, Charles. She was just impatient to be with her sister." Angela patted Millie affectionately. Millie smiled, leaned forward and kissed her baby sister.

Charles gently laid the tiny Dolores back into her cradle. "Oh Angela, how I have missed you! I have so much to share with you. I have made so many decisions without your wise counsel, and I hope they are right decisions."

With that, Charles lay beside Angela and began to tell her of his trip. He told her that it was a two day journey down to Concord in Carolina. He explained that the terrain was different, and then described the vast fields of cotton and tobacco. He told how these fields were worked by slaves...many, mere children.

He spoke of the young mulatto boy owned by Mr. Hathaway and he told her how the boy could read and work with numbers. He explained how helpful Dr. and Mrs. Rogers had been while he explored the new place and struggled to make his decision. Then he told Angela about Concord and the sacrifices they would make in moving from a thriving city like Richmond to a small community with only a general store from which to buy supplies. He told her about the God-fearing people and the outlying churches, and the school that was in the home of an elderly teacher. And he spoke of the kindness of the citizens and how eager and appreciative they would be to have a doctor living in Concord. Charles also explained that Concord was a poor community and people often used the barter system to pay for services and goods. He was brutally honest about the circumstances in which they would find themselves.

Then he said, "Angela, I accepted the citizens' enthusiastic pleas to move to Concord and become the village physician. Now I am having second thoughts.

Without your input I have made life-changing decisions. Living in Concord would be quite different from living in Richmond. The distance between the two cities is a two day journey. We would be leaving behind life as we know it for a life that will be completely foreign to us. So I'm asking you, have I made a big mistake? Should I have abandoned this foolish venture and remained here where life would be familiar, simpler, and most certainly easier?"

Angela had held Charles' hand during his entire narrative. She had not said a word. Now she reached up, drew his face to her, and kissed him softly. "Charles, darling, as far as the hardships of living in a challenging situation, we always knew this kind of venture would not be easy. If you want to help the needy, we must live where the needy live. That I would regret leaving Richmond is a groundless fear. You are needed in Concord and you are wanted there. Go. Go. Isn't this what you have dreamed of ever since you decided to become a doctor?"

Waves of relief swept over Charles and he

hugged Angela to him. "Angela, my angel, you make it all seem right. I supposed there were apprehensions hiding beneath the excitement and I feared I had made an unwise decision for you and the girls.

"Now I must tell you of yet another decision. I employed a carpenter to build a home for us. It will be on Main Street in Concord and my office will be attached to the house." Then he told her of the unfinished house, of the carpenter who could neither read nor write, and how the house would be finished by springtime.

"Oh Charles, our own home! I can hardly wait. Did you hear that Millie? Papa bought us a house...a house in North Carolina," said Angela.

Millie looked up from the baby she had been watching. A look of apprehension crossed her face. "Can we take her? Can we take our new baby?" she asked.

Angela and Charles smiled. "Of course, Millie,

we most certainly shall take Dolores with us."

Suddenly Charles felt flattened. He lay close to Angela and rested his head on her pillow. "I'm so tired, Angel," he said. "I was so concerned that I had not made wise decisions. It is such a comfort for me to know that you agree. Now, perhaps I can rest."

"Lay with me, Charles, and rest. Finally we are all together again," said Angela. But Charles did not hear her. He was sound asleep. Soon Millie curled up against Charles. Angela smiled and closed her eyes too.

& & &

"Dr. Charles, Dr. Charles," a whisper impinged on his rest. It was the nurse. "Dr. Charles...Dr. Edward, Dr. Robert, and your grandfather would like you to join them in the library."

Charles stirred and pushed himself up, being careful not to disturb his three beautiful girls. "Tell them I shall join them soon," he said.

This was the meeting Charles dreaded. He would tell his father about his decision to move to North Carolina and the circumstances under which he would live and practice medicine. He dreaded the questions and the criticism his father would hurl at him. He had been prepared to answer any questions that Angela might have, but his father made it difficult to defend his decisions. He wished to avoid more conflict with his father but after years of intimidation he realized that was unlikely.

Charles slipped quietly out of the room. As he walked across the balcony to the stairway, he stopped before portraits of two women. The younger of the two was Charles' mother. Her smile was kind and reassuring. She had golden hair, fair skin, and green eyes. Charles realized how much she and Angela looked alike. How would she feel about his leaving this home...the place he'd been born and the place she'd died giving birth to him? He did, however, know how the woman in the other portrait would feel. It was a portrait of his grandmother. She had cared for Charles after his mother's death. And while his father was away it was she who encouraged him to take risks and to be adventurous. How he wished they were here.

Charles continued down the steps and into the library. "Well, Charles, will you have a brandy?" his father said. Charles noticed he was already pouring him a glass.

"Yes Father, I'd like a brandy very much," said Charles hoping the drink would help make the meeting less unpleasant. Charles turned to his grandfather who sunk into the wingback chair in front of the fireplace. "Good evening, Grandfather," he said and lifted his glass in a toast.

Grandfather nodded, took a sip of his drink, and said, "I'm glad to see you made it home safely from your trip. I am most anxious to hear of your adventures."

"As are we all, Charles. Let us sit down, and you can tell us how you found North Carolina," Dr. Edward Singletary said.

They sat and all eyes were on Charles. He told them about Mr. Hathaway's hospitality and the amazing mulatto who could read and work with numbers. He told them about the town of Concord with one general merchandise store. He described how the citizens were ecstatic at the possibility of having their own doctor. Then, he described the house on Main Street. He told them he had bought the house and it would include his office. The room suddenly fell silent.

His father set his glass on the table, looked sternly at Charles, and said, "Then, we are to assume that you have already made your decision to move to Carolina and start your practice there without consulting your family?"

"Father, I have consulted my family. Angela and I are in agreement that this is what we want. You must have known when I made the trip that this might be our

74

decision."

"No, I did not," said Edward. "I thought that once you visited the place and assessed the situation, you would see that moving there would be a terrible mistake."

Robert angrily said, "How could you possibly choose Carolina over our family practice?"

"Quiet Robert," said Edward. "I shall handle this…"

Suddenly from the direction of the wingback chair by the fireplace a loud ***bang, bang.***

The startled men turned in that direction. Grandfather was banging his gold-handled cane on the floor. "There's nothing to *handle,*" he shouted. "The decision has been made and Charles made it. If it is a mistake, then it is his mistake. Now let us go in to dinner." And he slowly stood and started to the door.

Charles wasn't sure, but he thought he saw his

father's eyes fill with tears.

Robert approached Charles. His face was red and contorted with anger. "You've hurt our father very deeply. I hope your decision is worth it and that you can live with its consequences."

PART II

Our Very Own Home

Chapter 7

A warm spring breeze rustled the small green leaves of trees that lined the rutted road. Little buds erupted from branches that appeared to be dormant. Birds fussed and vied for the most desirable spot to build a nest. Baby chicks peeped behind mother hens and hogs suckled their piglets in pens behind the houses on Main Street in Concord, North Carolina. Barefoot children ran about, delighting in the energy and freedom they felt as cool dirt leached between their toes.

Suddenly a muddy, freckled face boy raced down Main Street toward the center of town. "They's comin'," he yelled. "Wait'll ya see. They's comin'."

Heads turned toward the top of the hill and people slowly moved in the direction the boy pointed. Then, topping the hill was a sight not yet imagined by the citizens of Concord. A barouche Carriage pulled by a beautiful white horse appeared. Perched upon the driver's seat was one whose arrival they had awaited since the previous fall...Dr. Charles Singletary. Beside him sat a lovely golden-haired woman and she was holding a baby. In the seat behind them, a young girl with long red curls bounced from one side of the carriage to the other squealing and waving with delight. Following behind the carriage were three wagons pulled by mules. The wagons were tightly covered, thus depriving the curious crowd of seeing its contents. The caravan stopped in front of the newly completed house on Main Street. Dr. Singletary carefully assisted his wife from the carriage, and then lifted the wiggling red-haired girl from the back seat.

Dr. Singletary turned to the crowd and announced, "Friends, we have finally arrived." Cheers and applause arose. When the crowd quietened, he added proudly, "This is my lovely wife, Angela. Angela will assist me in my office." Then placing his hand on the head of the red-haired girl, he added, "And this lovely young lady is my daughter, Mildred. We call her Millie." Millie grasped the hem of her skirts, bowed her head, and curtsied low. Dr. Singletary continued, "And this precious bundle is our latest blessing, Dolores. She will be called Lori."

Dr. Singletary shook hands and graciously received the greetings and welcomes of the townspeople. Women cooed over the baby and admired Angela's lovely dress. Such finery was seldom seen in small villages in eastern North Carolina.

The village children shyly approached Millie, who immediately began to chatter. Much to the amazed children, this new-comer quickly dominated the conversation. Then she sat down on the ground, removed her shoes, took off her socks, and stood barefoot in the road. It became quickly apparent that Millie would become a playground leader.

Finally, Dr. Singletary turned and eyed Mr. Davis who built his house. He stood silently, nervously apart from the rest of the crowd. Dr. Singletary looked directly at him, smiled encouragingly, and said, "Now

Mr. Davis, would you please escort us through our new home?" Mr. Davis immediately straightened, and with an air of new-found confidence, he led the doctor and his family up the crushed shell walkway to the steps of their new home.

Barefoot Millie had difficulty walking on the walkway but she soon scrambled up the steps and raced toward a swing that hung from the ceiling of the wrap-around front porch. Dr. Singletary noticed a small sign with an arrow pointing toward a side entrance to the house.

"Look, Angela we have a board," Dr. Singletary said. The sign read *To Doctor's Office.* Dr. Singletary wondered who had printed the sign. He recalled being told that Mr. Davis could neither read nor write. When Mr. Davis reached the front door he raised his hand to bring attention to the glass in the front door. "Lead," he said proudly.

"How lovely!" exclaimed Angela. "Just look, Charles! Why Mr. Davis, where on earth did you get that glass?" Mr. Davis just smiled.

He opened the front door and stood aside. Millie pushed past them and rushed into a large hallway. A carved staircase curved up two landings to the second floor. Millie soon climbed up to the first landing.

"Look Mama. See how high Millie is," she shrieked as she bounced up and down on the landing.

"Careful Millie, you mustn't run on the stairs," Angela said.

To the right of the hall was a parlor with a fireplace built of river rocks hauled in from the Roanoke River. Windows looked out over the front yard and Angela imagined lovely flower beds and ornamental shrubs placed tastefully along the walkway and in beds on the sides of the yard.

Beside the parlor, pocket doors opened into a large dining room where glass-fronted cabinets stood on each side of another fireplace. The dining room fireplace was also made of river rock and shared a chimney with the parlor fireplace. Bay windows provided the perfect spot for a serving table, and a chair rail ran along the walls encircling the entire room.

The kitchen was behind the dining room. It featured a large wood-burning stove with a wood box already filled with chopped wood. Shelves lined the walls, and wooden pegs were placed strategically behind the back door. The room had a long-handled water pump, and the sink was equipped with a drain pipe that carried water from the sink into a small ditch beside the back porch. The kitchen door opened onto a large porch where stone steps led down into the back yard.

"Mr. Davis, I am absolutely speechless!" said Angela. "You have thought of everything. Charles, isn't this amazing?"

Charles appeared to be pleased, yet Mr. Davis felt anxious. He sensed something had not fully met with Dr. Singletary's approval. Mr. Davis spoke nervously, "Doctor, would you like to see your offices?" And he hurried back inside.

They walked back into the front hall. Mr. Davis went immediately to the left side of the hall and opened pocket doors leading into another part of the house. They stepped into a room which had an outside door, and beside the door was another sign that read *Waiting Room*. At the far end of the waiting room, Dr. Singletary saw another door and moved quickly toward it. That door opened into what would become Dr. Singletary's private office. Here shelves reached from floor to ceiling and a window overlooked the back yard. An adjoining room would be his examining room.

Dr. Singletary slowly, carefully inspected everything in the three rooms. The waiting room was spacious and bright. Sunlight streamed through large windows that faced the front and side yards. Windows also allowed much needed sunlight to lighten his private office and the examining room. Dr. Singletary was speechless. Mr. Davis watched him apprehensively.

Finally Dr. Singletary turned to Mr. Davis, smiled, and said, "Mr. Davis, you have done yourself proud. What an incredible job. Thank you. Thank you very much." And he clasped the old man's hand and shook it vigorously.

"Who printed the sign?" Dr. Singletary asked motioning toward the waiting room sign.

"My son," Mr. Davis answered proudly. "My son is not witless like me. My son can read and write."

Dr. Singletary gasped. "Mr. Davis you most certainly are not witless. Just look what you have built." And he waved his hand about the room. "No witless man could have built this."

Tears rimmed the old man's eyes. "Thank you, Doctor. Your approval makes me proud… comin' from an educated man like you."

"Now if you will, sir, I am prepared to pay you for your extraordinary work," and he reached for a pouch tied around his waist, removed a large roll of bills, and counted out the dosh as Mr. Davis looked on delightedly.

"Next I would like you to build a small barn for my horse, a smokehouse, and storage shed in the back," said Charles.

Mr. Davis was ecstatic. "Yes sir, thank you very much, Doctor Singletary," he said. "You shall have the best outbuildings in Concord."

"I have no doubt of that, sir," said Dr. Singletary.

Then from the front hall they heard Mille call. "Mama, Papa! Come upstairs quick. I found my room!"

"Yes, dear, I am coming," answered Angela from the foot of the stairs. "I must see all the upstairs rooms."

Chapter 8

Life in the Singletary home on Main Street seemed complete. Dr. Singletary was so busy that he marveled how Dr. Rogers had ever been able to serve the patients in both Concord and his hometown, Jackson. Dr. Singletary had patients who had never been to a doctor nor taken medicine other than root and herb home remedies.

House calls were necessary for many of his patients, and Dr. Singletary was astonished at how often people became ill at night. Yet, home visits gave him insight into the meager lives of some of his patients. Many winter nights Dr. Singletary entered homes that were unheated and children slept together in an effort to stay warm. Wildlife and kitchen gardens were their main sources of food.

Birthing took place at home and on these calls

Angela accompanied her husband. Usually she carried along a sack of food or clothing the girls had outgrown. And, as Dr. Rogers had cautioned, Dr. Singletary's pay was seldom commensurate with his service.

Angela worked with her husband in many other ways. She kept records, ordered medications, and assisted in the examining room. If occasionally a baby were born in Dr. Singletary's office, Angela again assisted in the delivery. Whether at home or in the office she found being present at the time of birth to be a fascinating, almost sacred experience.

As Millie grew older she became more and more curious about her father's work. Charles and Angela laughed that the office was the only place Millie wore shoes. She entertained his waiting patients with her chatter and charm. If the patient were a child, she entertained the child in such a way that seeing the doctor was not a frightening experience. Soon Millie was no longer happy just helping out in the waiting room and it became difficult for Charles and Angela to keep her out of the examining room.

"Ah, Dr. Singletary," a patient once said, "'Tis too bad Millie is a girl. She would make a fine doctor."

Dr. Singletary thought to himself, "If Millie wants to become a doctor, being a girl won't stop her."

Millie and Lori flourished as they roamed freely about Concord with their friends. As was the custom, with the first hint of springtime, Concord children shed their shoes. Dr. Singletary joked with Angela that their girls had become part of the "barefoot brigade". The townspeople knew the Singletary girls well and Millie and Lori had visited every house and knew everyone's name. There was hardly a home in Concord that Millie and Lori had not been invited into because neighbors were curious about the girls and prodded them about the goings-on in the house on Main Street.

A genteel lady, Mrs. Fincher, who had once been a school teacher, opened a small school in her home. She taught reading, writing, arithmetic, geography, history, and the Bible. The students learned the Lord's Prayer. Faded maps of far-away places hung from the wall, and a wooden world globe could be turned unsteadily in its rusty metal stand. The students learned to recite poems with odd words about places they'd never heard of. The books were old and smelled dusty, and many were covered with smudges and had missing pages. Some students who lived on farms outside the village stayed in upstairs rooms in Mrs. Fincher's home during the school week and returned to their homes on the farm on the weekend.

Learning reading and solving arithmetic problems were simple tasks for Millie. However, she often lost herself in stories about ancient people and places. She would find the places on the faded world maps and wooden globe and dream of traveling to these places where Mrs. Fincher said history was born.

Lori excelled in reading. Unlike Millie, she preferred to read stories about brave knights, fire-breathing dragons, and battles to save lovely maidens. But most of all, she loved poetry. Lori soon began to try her own hand at writing poems and received much praise and recognition for them. At night, she and

Angela sat alone and Lori recited her poems. Angela cherished those quiet moments alone with her daughter, the dreamer. She marveled at Lori's ability to write poetry. One year, Lori memorized more poems than anyone in her class and became known as the class poet.

Lori also had another skill. She wrote her letters using a style much like that of ancient scribes. Mrs. Fincher was amazed at her exquisite script. So, whenever announcements or invitations were sent home to parents, Lori was asked to use her extraordinary talent to create a very special letter.

Unfortunately, Lori struggled with numbers, and this resulted in many hours of coaching by her father. This was a daunting experience. She would sit for hours at the long dining room table as Dr. Singletary patiently tried to come up with different ways to explain these problems that were so perplexing to Lori.

& & &

One morning in 1831, while Angela stood in the kitchen she distinctly felt the house shake. At first she thought it was her imagination. Then in a few minutes it shook again. The second shaking was followed by an earsplitting noise. Angela dropped the pan she was scrubbing and ran toward Dr. Singletary's waiting room. It was apparent from the looks on the faces of the waiting patients that they too had felt the vibration and heard the noise. Angela burst into his office, "Charles, I think we're having an earthquake," she shouted.

Charles shook his head and smiled broadly. "My dear, have you forgotten your childhood sounds of the city? That wasn't an earthquake. That shaking was caused by a train. The Seaboard train must have arrived." Charles' explanation was abruptly followed by yet another shrill whistle. Angela covered her ears.

At that moment the front door burst open and Millie and Lori rushed in. "Mama, Papa, the Seaboard train is here. Come look!" Millie was ecstatic as she bounced up and down. "Come! Please let's go see our train."

Lori, however, did not share her sister's enthusiasm. She was overawed and shook with terror. Tears rushed down her cheeks. She did not share Millie's curiosity for the giant machine. She sobbed, rushed to a corner of the waiting room, crouched down on the floor, and curled into a ball. Angela and Charles rushed to Lori and knelt to comfort her. "Lori, Lori," Charles whispered. "There's nothing to be afraid of. That loud whistle is saying 'Concord...I'm here. Seaboard Railroad finally sent me'."

Angela said, "Lori dear, we are all here and we're not afraid. If the train could harm you, wouldn't we all be afraid?"

Millie explained loudly, "Lori doesn't like loud noises. She started crying and the others teased her. I told them to hush up. She's not a baby."

"I'm proud that you defended your sister, Millie. Now we must do something about Lori's fear." Charles stood, reached down to Lori, and pulled her upright. "Come Lori. Come with me. We are going downtown to see the Seaboard train."

Dr. Singletary apologized to his waiting patients. He explained that he must go with his family to show them that a train is nothing to be frightened by and invited them all to accompany them.

Lori clutched Dr. Singletary's hand firmly as the family and the waiting patients paraded together down the hill toward the railroad tracks. A crowd had gathered around the train and the engineer entertained the people by blowing short whistle blasts. Lori's grasp on her father's hand slowly loosened, and soon she was laughing and jumping around without restraint.

A townsman approached the Singletary family. "What do you think of our train, Doc? Ain't she something? Why, I bet there ain't a finer one this side of the Mississippi. What do you say?"

"I say it is indeed a fine train, Mr. Wheelwright," said Dr. Singletary. "Yes, it is something for Concord to be proud of."

"Sure is," said the wheelwright. "Why, I could hop on that train right now and be in Portsmouth, Virginia, before day's end."

Several men who overheard their exchange approached to enter the conversation. "Aren't you afraid folks might not need your services any longer, Sir?" said the owner of the general store to the wheelwright.

"Not a bit afraid," answered the wheelwright. "Don't recall ever having a'body order wheels because they're driving their wagon to Portsmouth."

An astute gentleman dressed in a suit and vest approached. "So, Dr. Singletary, do you think things will change now that we have a train running through our town?"

"Yes, Mr. Adams, I do," replied Charles. "I most certainly think there will be changes in our town."

Another citizen overheard the men's exchange, ambled over, and said, "Doc, some of us have been discussing ways this train could revolutionize Concord. Now, I'm of a mind that we'd enjoy even more benefits if we changed the town's name from Concord to Seaboard in honor of the railroad company. So what's your opinion, Dr. Singletary?"

"Gentlemen, gentlemen, I shall leave such high level decisions to you. I will just say that I would not be averse to such a change," said Dr. Singletary.

Chapter 9

So, the village's name was changed from Concord to Seaboard in honor of the Seaboard Railroad Company and in appreciation for benefits derived from it. And the people indeed reaped small benefits from the train passing through their village.

A fish market was built behind the general store and fresh salt-water fish were brought in daily from the Atlantic beaches. To the delight of the villagers the fish were so fresh that they sometimes flopped about in crates of ice. The children rushed to the fish market when they heard the train's afternoon whistle. As the fish-monger opened the crates he told the children the names of the fish and pointed out their identifying characteristics.

The villagers no longer felt so isolated. Now they

could visit family and friends along the line whom they had not seen in years. Family and friends, in return, visited Seaboard. Soon, a two story wooden hotel was built beside the railroad tracks providing rooms for visitors. Home-cooked meals were served and occasionally, villagers would enjoy a meal in the hotel dining room. The large dining area provided other accommodations. On the first Monday of every month, the dining room was closed and used as a meeting hall for the Seaboard Masonic Lodge.

The general store increased its inventory to include long sought-after items. The basket of used shoes was replaced by boxes of shiny new shoes of different sizes and types. A greater variety of fabric replaced the dusty, shaded cloth on the tables and a selection of paper patterns featuring a variety of the latest styles excited the village seamstresses.

Dr. Singletary also benefited from the improved economy. Now his services were paid for in cash instead of produce and livestock.

Life in the Singletary household also progressed smoothly. Soon, Lori and Millie were lovely young ladies and their attention was much sought after by the young men of Seaboard.

Millie was a replica of her father. She not only inherited his ruddy complexion and thick, curly red hair, she also had a passion for caring for the sick. Millie was confident, dependable, and day or night she accompanied her father on house calls. Doctor Singletary quickly grew to depend on Millie even in the most challenging cases.

Second daughter, Lori, was more like her mother, Angela. Lori was imaginative, sensitive, soft-spoken, and still spent hours with her mother reading poems, plays, and fairy tales. Life in the Singletary house seemed serene and complete. Charles no longer harbored doubts about his decision to move to Seaboard.

Although Angela no longer accompanied Charles on house calls, she continued to assist him in the office.

She was his friend, wife, and the mother of his two lovely daughters. Then, sixteen years after the birth of the younger daughter, Lori, Angela and Doctor Singletary were stunned to find that Angela was pregnant again. Angela viewed her pregnancy as a miracle, and Doctor Singletary was delighted to see his wife so happy. However, he was apprehensive.

"Angela, it has been sixteen years since you carried a child...sixteen years since you delivered a baby. I am concerned for you. You must be careful. I don't want you to work in the office. Millie is quite capable there, and Lori will take care of you. Let her do..."

"Charles, Charles," Angela raised her hand and covered his mouth. "Much older women than I have babies. You know that. Please don't worry."

Weeks later, when the Doctor detected two heart beats, Angela wept with joy. Miracles...her two miracles. Charles, on the other hand, grew more concerned than ever. He realized that carrying two babies would cause more stress than carrying a single child. Charles was determined that Angela receive the best care. He was confident that Lori and Millie could care for their mother with love and devotion during her pregnancy and after the delivery; however, he needed medical reassurance. So he called upon his old friend and mentor, Dr. Rogers, to assist him in taking care of his wife.

Months went by without problems. Then summer arrived. Sweltering summers in eastern North Carolina can be brutal, and this summer appeared to be particularly hot and humid. As her time drew near, Angela became more and more lethargic. Her hands and feet swelled, and even cold baths lovingly administered by Millie and Lori did nothing to reduce the swelling. Lori spent hours fanning Angela, but this served only to stir the sweltering air. With the heat came loss of appetite. Angela's eyes became sunken and her fair skin grew ashen. Doctor Singletary became increasingly alarmed.

Dr. Rogers advised that the only way to reduce

swelling was to perform a bloodletting and he recommended it be done before the onset of labor. Doctor Singletary was unconvinced. He had recently read a medical opinion questioning the practice of bloodletting. In fact, he learned that many modern doctors claimed it was detrimental, even deadly to the patient. Doctor Singletary shared this new information and his concerns with Dr. Rogers.

Dr. Rogers argued, "Bloodletting has been used in this country since it was brought on the Mayflower. Are you questioning a practice that was used to treat our first president, President George Washington?" Dr. Rogers repeated his strong conviction that bloodletting was vital for Angela's well-being, and the sooner it was done the better. Reluctantly Doctor Singletary agreed.

So one hot morning in July, Dr. Rogers arrived at the Singletary house carrying a cast brass case containing a scarificator. The scarificator was a dreadful-looking instrument used in bloodletting. The apparatus was cocked and a trigger released spring-driven rotary blades that made many tiny cuts. The blood from the cuts was caught in a shallow bowl. Dr. Rogers told Charles that draining sixteen to thirty ounces of blood was not unusual. Charles cringed. Then he looked at his beautiful Angela who was swollen and pale, and she smiled reassuringly. So they proceeded.

Millie and Charles recoiled as the trigger emitted a loud snap releasing the blades. What a horrible sound. They watched in horror as the shallow bowl slowly filled with Angela's blood. When the bowl was filled, Millie simply replaced it with another. Lori cried softly as she carried one bowl of her mother's blood after another to the kitchen and simply poured it into the sink. During the bloodletting, Angela fainted, and Dr. Rogers stopped the bloodletting. Dr. Rogers appeared not to be concerned and assured Charles that fainting merely indicated how badly she needed bloodletting.

Then on a sultry, rainy day toward the end of July, Angela went into labor. Mercifully, her labor was short. Dr. Singletary and Dr. Rogers delivered. Millie assisted, and Lori continuously comforted her mother, fetched clean linens and hot water, and did anything else needed. Surely Angela would begin to regain her strength now.

The first twin to arrive was a boy. He was red and wrinkled and looked like a little old man. He came with a lusty cry that warned everyone that he *would* be heard. He wiggled and squirmed and flayed his tiny fist in such a way as to alert every one of the challenge he would be.

The tiny girl arrived less vociferously, sucking her thumb. She was smaller than her brother and not quite so lively. Her cry was audible but not as demanding as her brother. She was pink and perfect, and tears of joy streamed down Angela's cheeks as she was handed to her.

"Give them to me," Angela pled, her thin arms reaching upward. "Please give me my *miracles*."

Lori and Millie cleaned the twins, wrapped them in soft blankets, and lay a twin in each of Angela's arms. When Charles looked at Angela's peaceful, smiling face, he was confident that Dr. Rogers' recommendation had been best for Angela.

The twins were given the names of Angela's parents. The baby girl was Wilhelmina. They would call her Willa for short. The raucous little boy was named Willis. How could two tiny babies bring such amazing joy to an entire family?

Doctor Singletary eagerly hurried home from house calls just to gaze for hours at his lovely wife holding their *miracles.* Millie and Lori vied for turns to care for the twins. And Angela spent hours lying awake staring at them and memorizing every feature of the tiny cherubs.

The family's joy was short lived, however. The twins failed to thrive. Angela simply did not have enough milk to feed two hungry babies. One afternoon, Lori and Millie tried to comfort the crying twins. Angela looked on fearfully with tears in her eyes. She felt so helpless. All of her efforts and pain would be for naught if she could not satisfy her babies.

"Millie," said Angela. "I cannot nurse our little *miracles*. I don't have enough milk to satisfy two hungry little babies. You must find a wet nurse. She must be someone who has just weaned a baby and her breasts are still making milk. She must have big breasts, Millie, for we have two hungry mouths to feed."

"Don't worry Mama," said Millie. "I know of a slave woman who has just weaned her two-year-old child. The slave belongs to Mrs. Adams. I'll go and speak to Mrs. Adams now. Surely she will allow us to borrow her until our babies are old enough to take sips of milk from a cup."

Millie handed Lori the twin she was holding and rushed out of the room leaving her sister with two wailing babies and Angela with tears streaming down her cheeks.

Angela soon fell asleep from exhaustion and the

twins cried themselves to sleep with thumbs in their mouth. Shortly Lori heard slow footsteps on the stairs. Millie entered the room first. Behind her walked a tall, fat, black woman. A shy frightened toddler of about two years tagged along behind.

"Mama," said Millie.

"Shh. She just fell asleep," said Lori.

Millie said, "Lori this is Wanda. She will be wet nurse for the twins. Wanda has been wet nurse many times. Haven't you, Wanda?"

Wanda did not answer. She simply walked to the rocking chair and sat down. She unbuttoned her shirt, lifted out her two large breasts already oozing milk, and reached for a twin. Then she reached for the other. Detecting the smell of milk the twins were instantly awake their mouths reaching for a nipple. Wanda motioned to her toddler to sit on the floor beside her. He stared curiously at the twins busy sucking his mother's breast. Then he sat, rested his head on her leg, and began to suck his thumb. Soon he was asleep. As Wanda rocked, she softly hummed a tune Lori and Millie did not recognize. She still had not spoken a word.

One evening, Charles rushed home and straight to Angela's room. He was shocked at Angela's appearance. It seemed that in a few hours her appearance had worsened drastically. Her thin, pale skin stretched tightly across her gaunt face. Her eyes were vacant and dull. Yet on each arm lay a twin. The babies squirmed and cooed and smiled at their adoring mother. Dr. Singletary rushed to her side and buried his face in her hair in order to stifle a cry.

"My darling," she said weakly, "I miss you when you go on a call. Look, see how they are growing."

Charles raised his head, smiled weakly, and said, "Yes, my Angel, they are growing well, but you look so weak."

"Angela," he said hesitantly. "I can't lose you.

Please stay with us." Then he burst into tears and lay his face down on her bed.

"Charles, please don't be so distressed? I shall be well very soon. Why, I already feel better than I did yesterday."

Charles raised his head and looked at his Angel's smiling face. Somehow he felt peace at her reassurance.

The family's joy was short lived, however. Angela remained pale and failed to regain her strength even after two more bloodlettings. Finally Dr. Singletary realized with horror that bloodletting was not helping Angela but was in fact draining the very life out of her. But it was too late. Day after day she just lay in bed, a *miracle* cradled in each arm.

Then one evening, Millie and Lori tiptoed into their mother's room to fetch the twins to their cradles. Dappled moonlight fell upon their mother's pale face, and her lips curled slightly into a peaceful smile. She laid quietly, a twin in each arm. Even before they reached down to lift the babies they knew their mother was dead.

& & &

It seemed that the whole village attended Angela's wake. Her body was laid out in a white coffin that Mr. Davis had lovingly built. Row after row of viewers passed through the Singletary parlor as Charles sat beside the casket, his arm gently lying on Angela's cold arm. He sat by her coffin night and day. His face was stoic and he was completely cried out. Anger surged through him as he recalled the brutal blood lettings intended to heal but served only to cause her pain and shorten her life.

Lori and Millie thanked the guests for coming, and invited them back to their home following their mother's burial. Then Millie and Lori walked over to the village builder. Millie said, "Mr. Davis, what a lovely coffin you built for my mother. She would be so pleased. She always praised your work."

Charles overheard Millie's comment, turned a pale face toward their voices and called to Mr. Davis.

Mr. Davis walked quickly to him with tears rolling down his cheeks. "I am so sorry…"

"I know. I know. But now I must ask yet another favor of you."

"Anything Doctor, I'll do anything for you. You need only ask," he said as he choked back tears.

"My friend, I now call upon you again to use your excellent building skills. I want you to build a grave house for my beautiful Angela. Build her a grave house with windows and a door so I can go inside and sit by her gravestone and be near her. Can you do that for me my friend?"

Mr. Davis could not speak. He just nodded.

"Good," said Charles. "Angela was so happy in this house you built, so I shall leave the details of her grave house to you. There is only one request, my friend. Please make it large enough that I too may someday join her there."

& & &

Following Angela's death, the family treasured the twins even more. Dr. Singletary continued to call them their *miracles* and, even before they were old enough to understand, he told them stories about their beautiful mother, who was now an angel watching over them. He also told them the love story of Charles and Angela. Willa sat wide-eyed, captivated by the romantic tale. Willis, however, giggled and thought such stories were silly and only for girls' entertainment.

Dr. Singletary loved his children and they brought him much happiness and helped ease the pain of Angela's death. While Angela was alive, Dr. Singletary did not want to leave her for even one night. However, following her death he had a need to soften the memories of their life together and as a family in the

112

big house on Main Street. Every room was Angela. Pictures smiled hauntingly, teasingly out at him. The flower beds she had planted continued to reappear each spring reminding him that she would never come back. He kept running across her personal items in drawers and he often thought he smelled her scent on their bed. Sometimes her presence was so intense that he could hardly breathe. He felt he could reach out and touch her.

In the past, Dr. Singletary avoided medical conventions because they took him away from his family...away from Angela. Now, however, he needed a respite. Perhaps a medical convention would provide a much needed diversion from his obsessive memories and painful reminders. He rummaged through his desk drawer and pulled out a letter containing information on the Southeastern Medical Convention to be held in Fayetteville, North Carolina. He searched for the date and was relieved that the deadline had not passed.

Chapter 10

Dr. Singletary drove on the high seat of his barouche carriage across one hundred and fifty miles of dusty, rutted roads from his home in Seaboard, North Carolina to Fayetteville, North Carolina. By the time he reached his destination he was sunburned and his entire body ached. His shoulders and arms actually throbbed after bending forward and grasping the horse's reins for so many hours. The trip had been hot, dusty, and exhausting. He coughed and blew his nose loudly in an effort to free his lungs of dust. Fortunately, he found that ordinaries posting clean beds and hot meals for worn-out travelers were conveniently located at intervals along the route. Most of these public houses also offered shelter and food for slaves and care for travel-weary horses.

Dr. Singletary attended the five-day medical conference which was held in Fayetteville. Since Angela's death, he actually felt relief to be away from a place that held such poignant memories. It had been two years and he missed her still. So when heartrending thoughts clouded his mind Dr. Singletary was disinclined to rush back to Seaboard. On a hot, dusty day he delayed his return home by wandering idly through the streets of Fayetteville toward a marketplace located in the center of town.

Charles had read in a brochure at his hotel about the Market House and the surrounding marketplace. When the State House burned in 1831, a Market House was built on its ruins using the same design as town-hall markets being built in England. A marketplace soon surrounded it.

Lining the streets were large wicker baskets filled with freshly picked vegetables still warm from the sun. From the backs of wagons, farmers displayed loads of cotton and corn. Chickens, geese, and pigs squawked and squealed and struggled helplessly to escape from makeshift pens. Merchants came from the coast to sell dried fish, live oysters, and clams. The clock in the Market House tower was only now chiming the breakfast hour, but the Square was already bustling with peddlers hawking their wares and shoppers haggling over prices.

Dr. Singletary continued to walk toward the Market House which was in the center of the square. A crowd was gathered around the House and the clean morning air was filled with excitement and curiosity. The doctor jostled himself to the front of the crowd and asked an onlooker what was going on.

"Ain't you heard, Sir?" the peddler said, "There's to be slaves auctioned this morning."

Dr. Singletary was then told that a plantation owner died and, after paying his debts, his widow was left virtually penniless. In order to raise money on which to live, she was selling all her slaves. Dr. Singletary found the concept of one human *owning* another abhorrent and the brutal treatment of some slaves inhumane.

He looked carefully about him and was appalled by what he saw. Slaves were shackled and held in a slave pen constructed of tall rails with wide planks nailed between them. Frightened eyes peered through the cracks between the planks. Then a hush fell over the crowd and the auction began. As a number was called, a slave was fetched from the pen and thrust onto the Market House steps where they were forced to turn for all to see while an auctioneer pressed the crowd to bid higher. Doctor Singletary was speechless as he witnessed this callous process.

A number was called and a young woman was grabbed from the pen. She looked to be about eighteen and was very thin. Her skin was a shiny, ebony tone. She wore long skirts of an indistinguishable color, and her hair was hidden under a kerchief. Her eyes were wide with fear, and tear tracks could be seen on her dusty cheeks.

Suddenly, a little girl of about two years old burst

117

from the pen, ran to the young woman, and grasped her ragged skirts. The child was mulatto. Her skin was so light that she could have passed for a white person who'd spent too much time in the sun. Her hair was course and platted in corn rows but a golden tinge portrayed her true roots. She was barefoot and dressed in rags.

"Mama, Mama," she wailed. The young woman grabbed the child and clung to her desperately.

The slave handler suddenly struck the woman squarely in the mouth with his fist. Blood spurted from her mouth and she began to crumble. Doctor Singletary rushed forward and grabbed her before she hit the ground. The child continued to wail and cling to her mother.

The auctioneer, fearful that attention would be diverted from the steps to the scene at the pen, attempted to move things along. He motioned for mother and child to be brought to the steps together. What a pitiful sight! The young woman stood on the steps with blood smeared on her face staring straight ahead in shock. With snot running from her nose, the small child stood beside her in a puddle of urine, and continued to bawl at the top of her lungs.

Dr. Singletary was overwhelmed. He had to do something. The auctioneer became distracted by the child's wailing and ordered that she be forcibly torn from the mother. Dr. Singletary could stand no more.

"No," he shouted. "I want to bid for them both. I want to buy the mother and child…together."

The auctioneer looked skeptical. He said, "Both of them? Together?" And he looked at the pathetic sight on the steps. "As you wish, sir," he said. Then he addressed the crowd, "What do I hear for the woman here and her mulatto pick-a-ninny?"

There were a few bids for the two on the steps, but bidders were more interested in strong, young men who could work in the plantation fields during the brutally hot North Carolina summers. So, much to

Doctor Singletary's astonishment he soon became a slave owner.

Stunned by what he had done, the doctor walked over to the penkeeper and asked what to do next.

The keeper looked at him bewildered, "You ain't ner bought ere slave before, sir?" he asked.

"No," Dr. Singletary said weakly. Then he became angry with himself. He was actually embarrassed at not having ever bought a slave. He quickly regained his composure and added impatiently, "Now direct me as to how to proceed."

The keeper instantly assumed a more deferential tone and told Dr. Singletary how to proceed. He must first pay for the slaves, receive a receipt, and then return to the pen to claim his property. Dr. Singletary did as instructed and soon found he was standing alone beside the black woman and her child. He looked at her dusty, blood-smeared face and then down at the bawling, wet baby clinging to her skirts. What would he do with this woman and her baby?

Dr. Singletary didn't know how to conduct himself so he commanded the woman, "Comfort your child." The woman blinked. She lifted the child, wiped her nose with her sleeve, and began to comfort her. As she rocked her baby back and forth, Dr. Singletary noticed her eyes were fixed on the slave pen. A young man stood staring intently through gaps between the boards. His shackled hands could be seen through the cracks, and he wiggled his fingers in a tiny wave at the woman. Tears ran down his cheeks.

"Who is that man?" demanded Dr. Singletary.

The woman looked at the ground and whispered, "He be's my husband."

"My God, I've torn apart a family," thought Dr. Singletary. Then he asked, "What is his name?"

"Abel," said the woman averting her eyes from the doctor.

"What is your name?" he asked.

"Bella," she answered.

"And her's?" the doctor asked, nodding toward the baby.

"Ain't got no name.   Jest calls her baby," said Bella.

Doctor Singletary recalled the hours he and Angela spent choosing their children's names, and this poor child had no name at all. He looked at her little hands, thin arms, and bare feet. She's was so thin that it was impossible to judge her age.

"Tiny," he said. "We shall call her Tiny because she's so small."

Bella looked confused, said nothing, and just blinked again.

"Now I must see about that young fellow," Charles said, nodding in the direction of the steps. Abel was being pushed up the steps, his eyes never leaving Bella. Dr. Singletary was soon bidding again. This time the doctor found his bid greatly challenged. Unlike the woman, farmers recognized a wise investment. They could get many years of work in the fields from this strong young man. With each bid, the frightened man looked pleadingly at the doctor. His beseeching look compelled the doctor to bid higher and higher.

Soon Dr. Singletary owned three human beings, and in so doing he felt he'd denounced one of his most strongly held moral convictions…his opposition to slavery. He was so repulsed by the sight and sounds and smells of the slave market, he wanted to leave immediately on his journey back to Seaboard. The penkeeper looked at Dr. Singletary in disbelief when he was told to remove Abel's shackles.

"He'll flee like a jack rabbit, Sir, and she'll be right behind him," said the penkeeper.

"Just do as I ask," Dr. Singletary snapped.

The keeper removed the shackles and handed them to the doctor. Dr. Singletary threw them on the ground. Then he turned and stormed away. He quickly realized that three frightened people scurried to keep up with him. When they were well away from the slave market, he stopped abruptly and was almost run over by the family. They were standing by a horse watering trough.

Dr. Singletary pointed to the water. "Here," he said to Bella, "wash yourself and the child."

Bella lifted the hem of her skirt, dipped it into the water and washed the child's face. Then she leaned over the trough and repeatedly splashed water onto her face. When she finished washing her face, she dried it with her sleeve. Her lips were cut and swollen. Dr. Singletary examined the injury.

"I am a doctor," he said. "I'll put a healing ointment on that cut when we get to my wagon." Then he turned to the man. "Do you know how to drive a wagon?"

"Yah, suh," said Abel.

"Good. Do you know how to hitch a wagon to a horse?"

"Yah, suh," was the reply.

"Good. I'll take you to the livery stable. While you hitch the wagon, I'll fetch my belongings," said the doctor. "I have to get away from this inhumanity." Then he was off with the three tag-a-longs racing to keep up.

Chapter 11

They rode until way after dark. Dr. Singletary directed Abel on the route that he'd traveled when he drove the wagon from Seaboard to Fayetteville. Dr. Singletary sat in the back passenger seat of the barouche while Bella and Tiny sat up front with Abel. The child sat quietly…head against her mother's shoulder with her eyes glued on the stiff passenger sitting behind them. Once Dr. Singletary wiggled his fingers in a wave at the child, and Tiny shyly buried her face in Bella's breast. Bella opened her shirt and let the child nurse. It was then that Dr. Singletary remembered they had not eaten all day.

"Abel," he said, "Stop at the ordinary just up the way."

"Yah suh," said Abel

After only a few miles Abel reined the horse into

an open space in front of a two-story clapboard house. A board read, *Rooms to Let.* Dr. Singletary climbed from the carriage and walked to the door. Then he realized the family was still sitting in the carriage.

He turned to them and said, "I'll see to a place for you".

The owner of the establishment knew Dr. Singletary very well. The doctor had stayed at his ordinary several times and once paid his bill by treating the owner's son who was ill with pneumonia. The owner was also quite aware of Dr. Singletary's aversion to slavery, and was astonished when the doctor requested lodging for three slaves…three slaves he'd bought in Fayetteville. First, the owner stared at him in disbelief. Then he began to taunt the doctor relentlessly. Other guests quickly joined in the banter calling him "mustah" and finally the whole room was in an uproar. Dr. Singletary took the mockery good-naturedly. Then, with tears of laughter rolling down his cheeks, the owner finally said the slaves could sleep on the hay in the barn, and he'd send blankets and food out to them.

"So you think they'll be there in the morning, Doctor?" asked another lodger.

Doctor Singletary groaned, "I almost hope they aren't. What shall I tell my family?"

The lodge-owner slapped his hand on the counter, threw back his head, and laughed boisterously.

Charles did not sleep well that night. Although he longed to see his two older daughters and the twins, he dreaded returning to the place that held so many happy memories of his time with Angela. He knew tender memories would haunt him…bitter-sweet memories. And how would Millie and Lori react when they learned he had bought three slaves? Would they question how deeply his convictions against slavery actually ran? Oh, to lose the respect of his daughters would be more than he could bear.

He also worried about Bella, Abel, and the child.

Were they warm enough sleeping in the barn? What would he do with them? How should he behave toward them? How would he care for them? What about clothes? Where were they to sleep? What work would they do at his home? Dr. Singletary had never owned a slave of his own. And, although he had grown up in a home with slaves he had paid little attention to the interaction between masters and slaves. He remembered the comment made by other lodgers that they might not be in the barn next morning, and again halfheartedly hoped they would be gone.

But next morning they were there, sitting on the front seats, carriage hitched, and blankets folded. Charles started to climb into the carriage. Suddenly the owner stepped out of the ordinary. "Dr. Singletary, Dr. Singletary, you forgot your lunch."

"Thank you," Charles walked back to the ordinary, reached for the basket, and whispered to the owner. "Did you pack enough for them?"

The owner threw back his head and laughed.

"Yes sir, Doctor. I did pack enough for *them.*"

Charles heard laughter from inside. Then someone shouted, "Doc, you got a lot to learn."

The journey required them to stay at two more ordinaries before reaching Seaboard. Now Charles felt more comfortable with his interactions with Abel, Bella, and Tiny. He was also more confident in requesting shelter and food for the family. He continued to be taunted by the ordinary owners and other lodgers about his new role as a slave owner but the remarks became less and less troubling.

For the remainder of the journey, Dr. Singletary rehearsed the explanation he'd give his family. What would they think of him? It pained him to think of losing their respect...of appearing to be less of a man than they thought him to be.

It seemed to Dr. Singletary that the rest of the journey went by too swiftly. Finally, after days of travel they arrived in Seaboard. As they approached

Main Street in Seaboard, heads turned and lips whispered as Abel drove the carriage straight through the center of town. The citizens of Seaboard had long known of Dr. Singletary's strong political opinions. Dr. Singletary had never tried to hide his disapproval of slavery. He leaned forward and gave Abel directions to his home at the top of the hill. Lori and Millie were working outside in flower beds in the front yard. They recognized the carriage trudging up the hill and raced out to greet their father. They stopped short when they saw the three strangers seated on the front seats of the carriage. They gaped at their father as he wearily climbed from the wagon.

"Papa?" they said together.

"Please, Lori, Millie. Not now. I must first see the twins. How are they?" he said.

"Well..." began Lori never taking her eyes off the three who still sat on the front seat.

"You can't imagine how they have grown in just

the short time you were gone. Yes, go and see the Miracles," Millie said more confidently.

"But Papa," said Lori, "what about…" And she pointed to the family in the wagon.

Dr. Singletary was already climbing the steps. "Millie, take care of them…clothes, food, bedding, what odd pieces of furniture you can put together. And have them clear out that storage shed. They can stay there. " He disappeared into the house and headed upstairs.

& & &

Abel, Bella, and Tiny settled effortlessly into the Singletary household. The out building was cleaned out for their cabin, and Lori found furniture in the attic…a bed, crib, two tables, stool, mirror, pitcher and bowl, an old chipped necessary pot, and chest. Millie assigned work to Bella and Abel, and Tiny tottered about freely in the backyard squealing and laughing.

Soon after their arrival, Dr. Singletary summoned Bella, Abel, and little Tiny to the office. Two strangers were seated in leather side chairs. Abel stiffened. Bella cowered. She'd learned a long time ago that men were not to be trusted. Little Tiny popped a thumb in her mouth and hid in her mother's skirts.

"Abel, this is the Sheriff Bland, Sheriff of Northampton County, and the other gentleman is the Honorable Judge Madison. They are both distinguished men in this county, and are friends of mine," said Dr. Singletary.

"Yes, suh," said Abel. Sheer terror surged through his body. Judge…Sheriff. No good could come from such an assembly.

"These gentlemen are here today, Abel, because I want to free you, Bella, and Tiny. I want the sheriff to witness this act, and the judge has drawn up the necessary documents," said the doctor. Abel looked confused.

"Do you understand what he just said, man?" asked the Judge with authority.

"No, suh," said Abel.

"What it means is that after these documents are signed by me and Dr. Singletary, you are no longer a slave. You will be free," said the judge. "Now do you understand?"

"Still, no suh," said Abel. "What's we 'spose to do?"

"You can do whatever you want to as long as you don't break the law," said the sheriff.

"No suh. Won't break no law. But where we gonna live?" asked Abel.

"Abel, you can live anywhere you want," said Dr. Singletary. "You may continue to work and live here if you like. In that case, I shall pay you a salary. It will not be a large salary, but I shall pay you."

"We stay har," said Abel emphatically. Bella nodded her head.

"Fine. Now let's get these papers signed. I've much to do," said the Judge impatiently. "Abel what is your surname...your last name?"

Abel looked confused. "Don't got no other name...just Abel. She be Bella and the baby, Tiny. No other name."

The judge hesitated and looked at Dr. Singletary. Charles nodded. The judge then said, "Abel freed slaves choose many different last names but often time they just take the name of their previous owner. What would you like to do?"

Abel did not hesitate. He said, "I like to take Dr. Singletary's name if it be alright with him." Charles nodded his head in agreement.

The judge reached for some papers, filled them out, signed them, and shoved them toward Dr.

Singletary to sign.

"Now you keep up with those papers, you hear?" said the Sheriff.

Abel just nodded. He was still dumbstruck. This was too much to comprehend so quickly. Later he'd ask the doctor to explain everything again.

The two visitors stood. As they prepared to leave each man extended a hand to Dr. Singletary. As they shook hands in turn, Abel noticed both men wore gold rings with the engraving of a square and compasses...just like the one Dr. Singletary wore.

Chapter 12

Life moved slowly for the citizens of this quaint village in Northampton County, North Carolina with the exception of the three fast moving children who lived in the two-story house on Main Street. Every day was an adventure for Willa, Willis, and Tiny. Their energy and imagination knew no bounds.

"Always look for them in unexpected places," Millie would say and shake her head in amazement. "...in the top of that tallest pecan tree, or hunting for turtles in the drainage ditch, or hiding from us in the attic. Yes, those are the places you will most likely find our *little miracles*."

And then Lori would say sweetly, "Yes, they are mischievous, but at night they sit so quietly, so attentively when I tell stories of Mama. They are like little cherubs." Millie simply rolled her eyes incredulously.

Willis grew up to be strong-minded and brimming with curiosity. His desire was not so much to please as to shock. Whether he was hanging by one knee from a tall tree branch or hiding garden snakes in his sisters' rooms, he was always plotting some mischievous prank. Willis grew to be tall with unruly dark hair, and a nose sprinkled with freckles. He exploded with energy, and most often won the village foot races. Willis was always the leader of whatever games he and the village boys played.

Willa, on the other hand, exhibited none of the rebellious and adventurous traits of her twin nor did she share his physical features. Willa was fine-boned and fair giving her a fragile appearance. Like her mother, Angela, she had golden hair, green eyes, and a turned-up nose that made her appear inquisitive. At a very early age, Willa showed a *special gift*. She claimed the ability to see things and know things that others were not aware of. Often when Lori told Willa stories about their mother, Willa professed to see Angela and talk to her at night. Soon news of Willa's gift of foreknowing spread through Seaboard. Although Willa's *gift* was discussed it was never ridiculed. The respect for Dr. Singletary also extended to his family. Soon Willa was asked to speak with villagers' dearly departed or give comfort to a friend who lost a loved one.

Unlike Willis, Willa aimed to please…especially her father. Willa was beautiful, intelligent, quiet, and sedate. She was the kind of young lady who was the answer to any young man's dreams. Unfortunately, Willa would come to realize that these qualities were hopeless if the young man she loved was not acceptable to her father.

& & &

When the traveling minister came to call on the Singletary family, he was accompanied by his son. The minister explained that his son was reading to become a

139

man of God, and home visits to church members were an important element of his training. The minister's very appearance was menacing. He was tall with broad shoulders, long arms, and large boney fingers. His face was thin with deep-set dark eyes that darted threateningly about the room. He gestured continuously, spoke at full volume, and glared caustically at his listeners as his large Adam's apple crept up and down his throat.

The son's appearance, however, was quite different. He was tall, with broad shoulders and a narrow waist and hips. He had a patrician nose, blond hair, blue eyes and a firm jaw. When he was introduced, he nodded first to Willa and her sisters then to Doctor Singletary.

"Miss," he said with a nod to each young woman.

Later, Lori mimicked the young man by dropping her voice an octave, nodding, and saying to Willa, "Miss." Nonetheless, the young man's pretentious behavior impressed Willa who had been protected from the guiles of flirtatious young men and she immediately fancied herself madly in love with him.

While Doctor Singletary was on house calls, the minister's son called on Willa. Although Millie and Lori did not approve, they reckoned this was a state of affairs best handled by their father. So, one evening upon the doctor's return home, he summoned Willa to the parlor. He forbade her to ever see the minister's son again, calling both father and son, "ill-mannered, ill-tempered, and ill-bred." Willa's attempts to dissuade her father were weak at best, but she reluctantly promised to never see him again. This would be the only promise to her father that Willa ever broke, as many clandestine meetings between the two lovers took place out of eyeshot of her father, her sisters, and the gloomy minister. The two lovers devised a method to communicate with each other. They hid written messages in the hollow of an old elm tree. Through these secret messages they designated the next place they would meet.

Chapter 13

Doctor Singletary struggled to meet the needs of his patients in the village of Seaboard as well as the needs of those who lived on nearby farms. Days were long, nights short, and there were the never-ending worries about Willis and Willa.

After one trying day, Dr. Singletary pointed his old horse toward Seaboard and the weary animal plodded slowly up the hill. Large gray clouds raced across the eastern sky in the predawn hours of the unsettled September day. The wind carried a cold chill, and the air was heavy with the threat of rain. A large harvest moon shone between the clouds as it slowly edged toward the horizon, ready to give up its luster to daybreak. The village of Seaboard was silent and enveloped in the gray haze of fog.

The tired, old horse appeared out of the mist and trudged slowly up the muddy, rutted road. The barouche carriage wobbled and squeaked noisily. The horse's breath was labored, and he exhaled small puffs of condensation. Heavy drops of dew rolled off the coach roof and dropped onto the driver's tall hat.

The doctor found it exhausting to drive the carriage after such a demanding day. Although he was a man of distinction, his ruddy face was now tanned by the sun and wind, and wrinkles radiated from the corners of his eyes. Even though age was no longer his friend, he was tall and strong as he leaned into the wind. His voice was robust and assertive yet it possessed a gentle tone as he uttered words of encouragement to the exhausted animal, assuring him that they'd almost reached the top of the hill. The reassurance was unnecessary, however, for the horse knew exactly where he was, and he knew where to go. He knew he'd soon reach the barn where he would be dried and a warm blanket thrown over his back. And he knew that fresh water and a bucket of oats awaited him. Finally, they reached the top of the hill. The driver pulled his collar snugly around his neck, snapped the reins, and clicked his teeth. The weary horse found new energy and trotted purposely toward the large white house on Main Street.

Oblivious to the driver, a shadowy figure tracked the carriage. A tall, barefoot young man wearing rags ran beside the road darting behind bushes, trees, and out-buildings to avoid being seen in the imminent arrival of first light. At the top of the hill he hid in the foliage of giant English boxwoods and watched intently as the carriage turned onto the path beside the large house on Main Street. As he stepped from his hiding place, a faint glow in the east caught the face of the watcher. In spite of the chill, his dark mahogany face was streaked with perspiration and tears. His black eyes were wide and frightened and never left the carriage. The wounds on his wrist and ankles left by the ropes that had mercilessly bound him throbbed and stung. Symbols. The symbols. He must find the symbols. As he ran he emitted a low whimper like that of a trapped animal struggling to free itself from a snare. Finally he reached the house and padded slowly across the backyard creating small clouds of dust in his wake. He raced toward an outbuilding and crouched low.

The rambling two-story house was dark and still. Its leaded windows sparkled with the reflection of the moonlight, and a wrap-around porch held high-back rocking chairs that invited passers-by to stop in and exchange the latest town news. It possessed an aura of comfort and serenity. Early mornings duties had not yet begun.

Doctor Singletary reigned in the old horse and slowly stepped down from the carriage. He stretched and rubbed his aching, lower back. He looked forward to a hot posset and the warmth of his own bed. He heard the click of a door latch and turned to see the welcome face of his servant.

"Ah, Abel," he said, "I welcome the end to this day. I feel as if I could sleep for days."

"Ya suh, Doctor Singletary. Ya wuz gone real late dis time," Abel replied. "Ya posset is hot and ya bed is warmed up right good."

Abel's skin was so black that it shined. Even though he was older now, he was still a strapping man although his hair and eyebrows were grizzled. His hands were large and calloused, and he spoke with confidence and genuine concern for the doctor. Abel reached for the horse's reins in order to lead him. The horse, however, did not need to be led for he'd already started in the direction of the barn.

"Where is Willis?" Charles asked wearily.

"He done gone with some other boys over to Jackson to hear some man talk 'bout joining the army," Abel hesitated. Then he added, "Doctor Singletary, dat boy done got plum strong-headed."

"I know," said Charles resignedly. "I know."

The doctor trudged exhaustedly up the steps to his chambers on the second floor, and hung his cloak in the walnut press. He found a welcoming fire in the fireplace, a hot pot of posset warming on the hearth, and the handle of a warming pan protruding from under the bed quilt. He removed his dusty clothes, put on his woolen bed clothes, filled a cup with the hot brew, and sat by the fire while sipping his posset. He began to relax. The warmth of the hot drink and the blazing fire made him drowsy.

His eyes wandered to the portrait above the mantle. It was an oil painting of his breathtakingly beautiful young Angela. Soft golden curls framed her lovely, fair face, and smiling green eyes stared lovingly back at the doctor. She wore a dark green silk dress cut in a fashion to reveal her creamy white shoulders and firm youthful breasts. Her pale hands held a lace fan, and a heart-shaped ivory pendant was attached to a gold chain around her neck. Her impish smile invited him to remember some secret or memory shared only by the two of them…Angela…his angel.

Doctor Singletary looked at the portrait above the mantle. She smiled lovingly at him. He lifted his cup of posset, sighed, and said, "My dearest Angela, how I've missed your wise counsel over the years," then he smiled and added, "And I miss your presence in my bed."

The Doctor reached for a taper lying on a nearby table, lit it from the fireplace embers, and touched it to a candle on the table beside his bed. Suddenly a small flame flickered and shadows danced on the walls. He removed the warming pan and fell into his bed. The night candle burned warmly, throwing rays of light onto the heavy bed curtain. He adjusted himself comfortably and prepared to sleep. But sleep would not come easily.

Finally Doctor Singletary fell into a hard sleep and thought he had been sleeping for hours, but the sound of hurried footsteps jolted him awake.

"Papa, Papa, come quickly."

Doctor Singletary forced himself awake and looked into Willa's terrified eyes. "Willa, why are you here?" he asked.

"Papa, Millie says you must come at once. This one is badly hurt. Please hurry."

Doctor Singletary did not ask *who* was badly hurt. He knew that such late night emergencies most likely meant one thing...a slave was running. He flung back his covers, swung his bare feet onto the cold floor, and raced across the room to the dusty pile of clothes beside the hearth. He dressed haphazardly and was soon dashing down the steps and out the back door.

Outside he found Lori, Millie, and Abel bent over the still body of a young black man. Willa stood apart with a look of horror on her face.

"Go inside, Willa," barked Doctor Singletary as he knelt beside the lifeless form. The young man's hand stretched out toward a large stone. On the stone was carved the symbol, the Masonic square and compasses.

"Is he alive?" asked Doctor Singletary.

"Yah suh," replied Abel. "But jes barely."

"The man's been beaten terribly," exclaimed Millie. "And look at the rope burns on his wrists and feet."

"It's a sin, Papa," said Lori, "a *mortal* sin."

A crimson glow inched above the horizon in the east, and a cock crowed persistently, anxious to be turned out of the chicken house.

"Get him to the safe room at once. Help me, Abel," said Doctor Singletary. Then he realized that Willa was still standing there. "Willa," he cried, "I told you to go inside…this moment."

Willa looked crest-fallen. "Please, Papa," she pleaded. "Please let me help. I can do it. I know I can."

Doctor Singletary looked at Millie. Millie nodded. "Very well," said Doctor Singletary. "Willa tear sheets for bandages…lots of bandages." Willa ran up the steps and disappeared into the house.

As Abel and Doctor Singletary lifted the man, he groaned pitifully. Then mercifully, he fell into unconsciousness. As they carried him past the kitchen door, Dr. Singletary saw Bella, already boiling pots of water and making broth. Willa and Tiny were tearing sheets into strips for bandages.

"We have a challenge here, Bella," said Doctor Singletary. "This poor creature is more dead than alive." Bella simply nodded. She had grown accustomed to such late night crises.

The doctor and Abel carried the man up the steps and into the doctor's chamber. They laid him on the floor beside the fire, and together they moved a large chest that stood against the wall. The doctor stepped on a small paddle that appeared to be a part of the woodwork and pushed against the panel. There was a grating sound as a portion of the wall opened slightly. Abel forced his fingers into the crack and slowly parted the panels. The doctor fetched a candle, stepped into the dark opening, and placed the light on a small table. Light filled the tiny room and a dank, musty smell permeated his nose. The room was sparsely furnished. There was a small cot spread with clean linens and two quilts, another crudely built table holding a water bowl and pitcher, two straight-back chairs, and a necessary pot under the bed. The only source of daylight was a small leaded window set high in the wall. Outside the house, this window appeared to be one of several such small semi-circular windows decorating the wall above the porch.

"Lay him on the floor," said the doctor. "We have to clean and bandage his wounds. Help me remove his clothes." The man was laid, still unconscious, on the floor. After removing his clothes, Abel and Dr. Singletary were stunned by the many scars on his body that showed years of abuse.

Millie and Bella brought in pans of hot water, and Lori followed with more bandages. Millie and Bella bathed him thoroughly. Dr. Singletary applied healing ointment and Lori covered the wounds with bandages.

Willa and Tiny were not allowed in the room.

"I'll be a-setting with him so as he won't be scared when he wakes up," said Abel. Abel had done this many times.

Dr. Singletary simply nodded and left the room. He closed the door, but was too exhausted to push the chest in front of the panel. He collapsed into bed too tired to undress.

"Could this day bring any more horror?" Doctor Singletary muttered rhetorically as he drifted into near unconsciousness.

& & &

Dr. Singletary was not sure how long he slept. He was vaguely aware of Millie, Lori, and Abel creeping in and out of the secret room. Once he opened his eyes to see Willa's sweet face leaning close to his as if she wanted assurance that he was still breathing. He managed a wan smile, closed his eyes, and drifted back into a deep sleep.

In the realm of sleep in which one has difficulty distinguishing between reality and dreams, Dr. Singletary heard the barking of hounds. How incredible! Hounds? The din was quickly followed by the scraping sound of furniture being moved and the scurrying of footsteps. When loud voices floated up the stairway, the doctor recognized one frightened voice as that of Willa. Alarmed, he bolted upright, swung hurriedly out of bed, and made a dash for the stairs.

He appeared in rumpled clothes on the back porch to witness the chaos taking place in his back yard. The malevolent minister sat upon a bucking, black horse. He waved his arms menacingly, and raved manically. He was surrounded by a pack of yelping, baying hounds that were worked into frenzy. Four mounted local ner-do-wells laughed at the ridiculous sight while the minister's shy, powerless son sat apart from the mob and stared helplessly at Willa.

"We have you this time, Doctor Singletary. Indeed, the hounds don't lie. They have led us straight to your door...the door of an abolitionist. We know it is true. The whole county knows you hide runaways and God has led us to you. Yes, to you...right to your own door. And we'll find the runaway and hang him right here in that tree." He pointed a boney finger at the large oak that Tiny, Willa, and Willis used to climb on hot summer days.

"You're a fool, preacher," Dr. Singletary replied angrily, "a damned fool. What makes you think God would help the likes of you hang another human being? If you come into my home, I promise you hell to pay."

At that moment, the door opened and a pungent smell wafted from the kitchen. Then Bella slowly appeared on the porch. She carried a large platter above her head and on the platter was a sumptuous, aromatic ham. The hounds immediately stopped barking, lifted their noses, sniffed, and made a dash for the porch. A table toppled. The platter crashed, and the pack of hounds snapped and snarled as they fought for a bite of the ham.

"Eek! Help!" squealed Bella, and she fled into the kitchen.

"See what your hatefulness has done! You invade my property, frightened my children and my servants. You threaten me and accuse me of that which you have no proof. In addition, you destroyed my dinner. I repeat you are a fool, preacher. You are a damnable fool who will most certainly rot in hell."

The minister's companions had not yet spoken. They were bent over and tears of laughter streamed down their cheeks. The minister's face was red. Large veins protruded from his long neck. His son still sat to the side, but Willa thought she saw a faint smile cross his lips. At that moment they heard rapidly approaching hoof beats, and suddenly Sheriff Bland and two men rode up.

"Well, Sheriff," said the doctor, "just see what this devil has done!"

The sheriff looked at the hounds that were now devouring the last scraps of the ham. The sheriff smiled a wicked little smile and said, "I see…why he's fed your supper to the hounds. How outrageous preacher…stealing a man's supper."

The preacher was so outraged that the doctor feared he'd suffer a stroke. "We are hunting the runaway slave, and the hounds led us straight to the house of this abolitionist," the minister sputtered.

"Or perhaps the hounds led you to the kitchen with the most delicious smell," said the sheriff. His men laughed.

The preacher stammered, "You are not upholding the law, Sheriff. It is well known that this man is opposed to slavery. He is an abolitionist as sure as God is my witness. Search this place. Do your job."

The sheriff's face took on a dark expression. He spoke slowly, threateningly, "See here preacher, the last I remember, we are entitled to our beliefs in this country. No preacher man has changed that. As for my job, I don't need the likes of you telling me how to do it. Now get out of here and leave the good doctor and his family alone."

With that, the minister turned his horse and pulled up on the reigns causing it to rear up on its back legs. He called back, "Don't think this is the end of it. You'll pay for your sins…if not here, in hell." Then he galloped off with his pack of hounds following.

The sheriff slid down and walked over to Dr. Singletary. "Is *everyone* safe?" he asked.

"Yes, **everyone**," replied the doctor.

"When will the conductor arrive?" he whispered.

"I think tomorrow night. Bella hung out the quilt. But my guest is not able to run," said Dr. Singletary. "He must wait."

"That is dangerous," said the sheriff. "I'll try to keep a closer watch."

At that moment Bella walked back onto the porch and began to clean the clutter left by the hounds. "That was quick thinking, Bella," said the doctor.

"Too bad 'bout that ham though," said the sheriff.

Bella grinned. "Dat's jest one of them," said Bella. "The biggest one is jest 'bout ready to come out of the oven."

The sheriff rubbed his hands together and grinned. "Might I stay for dinner, Doctor?"

The doctor smiled and said, "You and your men are always welcome in my home."

Part III

The War

Chapter 14

1861

Every day Abel fetched newspapers brought in on the morning train. Sometimes they were two or three days old, but Dr. Singletary would shut himself away in his private office and search every paper.

Mail was also brought on the train. One letter from Brother Robert carried exceptionally sad news. Charles' beloved Grandfather, who had been Charles' benefactor in his most trying times, died and was buried in the family cemetery in Richmond. Charles was saddened that he was not with his grandfather at the time of his death, although he knew he would have discouraged him from leaving his medical responsibilities to make the long journey.

Robert also enclosed documents verifying that Grandfather left Charles a generous portion of his estate. This bequest only heightened Charles' feelings of guilt; however, he was relieved that Robert showed no resentment at Charles' inheritance.

Arriving by the same post was a letter from his father; as usual, his letters spoke exclusively of politics. He voiced uncertainty at the secession of southern states from the Union, and he also wrote of dissension among the citizens of western and eastern Virginia. Owners of large plantations in the eastern and southern parts of Virginia relied heavily on slave labor to tend the fields on their large plantations. These counties supported secession to continue using slave labor. However, in the western counties of Virginia, there were no large plantations that relied on slave labor and those counties saw no purpose in seceding from the Union in support of slavery. However, by the autumn of 1861, thirty-nine counties in western Virginia would vote to form a new state that remained loyal to the Union. The new state was named simply, "West Virginia", and at once it became a key border state in the war.

In North Carolina, a similar slave issue existed between the eastern counties with their large plantations that relied on slave labor, and western counties where there were no plantations and therefore no need for slaves. Accounts from the state Capitol, Raleigh, reported no possibility of a break between the eastern and western counties of North Carolina. In spite of their differences, it was strongly accepted that North Carolina would remain intact regardless of the secession decision. Events outside secluded Seaboard moved rapidly, and one morning Dr. Singletary opened his paper to read that on May 20, 1861, delegates convened in Raleigh and voted unanimously for North Carolina to no longer be a part of the United States of America. North Carolina had seceded from the Union, making it the last southern state to join the Confederacy. Dr. Singletary was stunned. Although he abhorred slavery he feared the consequences of secession. He thought of Willis, his son. His *miracle*. War!!! Willis in battle!!! Oh, Angela, our son!

Charles had read an earlier speech delivered by the strong president, Abraham Lincoln, in which he said, "A house divided against itself cannot stand. I believe this government cannot endure permanently half slave and half free."   Charles agreed with the President's sentiments, and he continued to allow his home to be used as a safe house on the Underground Railroad.

Then the dreaded happened.   One day Willis appeared wearing a gray uniform of the Confederacy, stood before his father, and saluted. "Private Singletary reporting for duty to the Confederacy, sir," he said. And his father simply wept. Dr. Singletary had prayed that his son would not fall for the fantasies being spun to lure young men into joining this wretched war. How he hated the war. How he hated slavery. But the deed was done…Willis was now a soldier in the Confederate Army.

"Papa, we'll be reporting in at Richmond, only a two day ride from here.   Perhaps, I can come home between battles," the naïve boy said in an attempt to reassure his father. Doctor Singletary simply continued to weep and held his *miracle son* tight to him.

Then one day there was a rat-tat-tat of drums. Willis proudly marched down Main Street of Seaboard with a group of gray-clad young boys. They waved, smiled, and shouted it would not take long to "finish the job". They would return home before Christmas. Dr. Singletary wept again as he watched the young boys march off like gray ghosts being consumed in the cloud of prophetic dust.

& & &

Every day Charles waited eagerly for Abel to return from the train station with the newspapers. Although the papers were often a week old, Charles' spirits were lifted as he read accounts of the war. Richmond newspapers reported triumphant battles in such places as Manassas (Bull Run) and the Shenandoah Valley in Virginia. The paper reported thousands of Yankees died while there were only a few hundred Confederate casualties. Dr. Singletary wondered if Willis had fought in those battles. He could not imagine Willis, his tender hearted, fun loving son, engaged in battle in which thousands of men died.

As the war progressed, communication from Northampton County soldiers painted a bleaker picture of the war than the newspaper accounts. They spoke of modest food rations, poor clothing, sleep in trenches infested with rats, and the constant gunfire. They told of the deaths of fellow soldiers, and the horrendous injuries the soldiers suffered. Despite these privations the letters indicated that the morale of the soldiers remained high and they had great confidence in the leadership of the army.

Dr. Singletary wondered if Willis ever received letters from him and his sisters. He longed to see his only son. He longed to hold him and protect him from the horror of this war.

Life in Seaboard became severe. The general population changed dramatically as all able-bodied men between the ages of fifteen and fifty enlisted as soldiers in the Confederate Army. Cattle, pigs, and horses were appropriated for the war effort leaving only old mules for plowing and one cow for each family with small children. Families gladly donated their food and warm clothing to their loved ones who were fighting so far away from home. They prayed their sons or husbands would benefit from such sacrifices.

One thousand Confederate soldiers were rural Northampton County "boys" and several camps were located in the county to train them. Troops trained at Camp Mangum, Camp David, and Camp Ranson in Northampton County and were considered to be the "best trained" in the Confederate Army. Because of its rich soil and skilled farmers Northampton also provided vital food and clothing for the troops. It was gratifying to the citizens to realize that their efforts were essential.

Northampton County was also crossed with railroads that moved much needed war supplies north to General Lee's troop in Virginia. However, these railroad links did not go unnoticed, and in July 1863

Union Colonel S. P. Spear and 5000 troops invaded Northampton County. Their mission was to march across Northampton and destroy the railroad bridge that crossed the Roanoke River thus disrupting a crucial link in the Confederate supply line. Confederate General Matt Ranson and two hundred Confederate troops were dispatched to Northampton County to halt their movement. General Ranson's troops engaged Spear's troops for three hours at Boone's Mill Pond. General Spear was eventually driven to Winton, North Carolina without accomplishing his mission to destroy the railroad bridge. This invasion by General Spear did nothing to quieten the nerves of the citizens. Even though General Ransom was victorious, the battle had reached their back door and their vulnerability became apparent.

& & &

In the spring of 1864, General Ulysses Grant launched a campaign to capture Richmond. Throughout the spring a series of battles began north of the city of Richmond and circled eastward ending south of

Richmond in early June.   The Siege of Petersburg had begun.

Dr. Singletary read everything he could find in the newspapers about the Petersburg Siege and the Confederate Army's efforts to defend Richmond.   A Raleigh newspaper's printed detailed coverage of these battles.   To Dr. Singletary's relief, it reported that the Confederate Army at Petersburg held firm their lines and General Grant's attempts to capture Petersburg and move on to Richmond were thwarted.

That was not, however, the end of the campaign. The railroad line between Richmond and Wilmington, North Carolina ran through the small town of Weldon, North Carolina and was a vital supply line for the beleaguered Confederate Army in Petersburg.   Weldon was a small railroad town on the Roanoke River only twelve miles from Seaboard. In order to isolate the Confederate Army defending Richmond, General Grant ordered a cavalry thrust south to capture and destroy a section of the Weldon Railroad and disrupt the Confederacy supply line. As the Union Soldiers advanced, troops under Confederate General William Mahone met the Union Cavalry near a point called Jerusalem Plank Road. (This would be called the First Battle of the Weldon Railroad.) Mahone was successful in driving the Union troops back but after a four day battle it was strategically a draw. The Confederates were able to retain control of the Weldon Railroad, but the Union troops immediately began to construct new trenches along the Jerusalem Plank Road.

So it was after this First Battle of the Weldon Railroad, that an appeal went out to all doctors remaining in the Weldon countryside. Most of the younger doctors were already away serving in field hospitals near the battlefields. The remaining older doctors were asked to volunteer as much time as possible at a makeshift Confederate hospital housed in the Methodist Church in the nearby village of Garysburg, North Carolina. Even though Dr. Singletary's age made the seven mile journey to Garysburg taxing, he offered his services. He reasoned that if he cared for young wounded soldiers at

Garysburg, then perhaps some doctor in Petersburg would care for Willis should the unthinkable occur.

With so many men away fighting, Dr. Singletary's Seaboard practice now consisted mostly of delivering babies, setting broken bones, and treating patients with illnesses such as pneumonia, consumption, and dysentery; so he was able to allot time to the Confederate Hospital as did other older doctors in the county. After all, he now had a personal empathy for the well-being of the Confederate soldiers.

On his first arrival at the hospital, Dr. Singletary was greatly impressed with the transformation of the small Methodist Church into a working hospital. A large sign was posted outside the church which read "Garysburg Confederate Hospital". Inside, pews were neatly pushed against the wall, and beds and cots spread with clean white sheets took their place in the sanctuary. Standing against one wall were large tables covered in white cotton cloth ready to hold medical supplies, medicine chests, and surgical instruments. The building was spotless and windows were open to allow a flow of fresh air.

Women from the village and the surrounding farms busied themselves about the church talking comfortingly to the few soldiers that were patients and redressing their wounds. People from town and nearby farms brought in good home-cooked food—breads, beef, chicken, fresh vegetables, fruits, and pies. Patients had been moved from the battlefield at Jerusalem Plank Road to Weldon by rail. They were then brought from the railroad to Garysburg in wagons piled with fresh hay and covered with clean bed quilts. Dr. Singletary was pleased at what he found and thought that volunteering his services here would not be so difficult after all.

On many occasions, Dr. Singletary had spoken loudly against this war as he had against slavery, but his opinion had not prevented North Carolina from seceding from the Union, although it was the last Southern state to do so. Now, circumstances had changed. He recognized some of the wounded as his friends, neighbors, and fellow citizens and moved quickly to comfort and to treat them. He hoped that his son would receive this same kind of care should he be injured. So, he reasoned he would serve until the two sides tired of their bickering and called a halt to this insane war. Surely that would happen soon.

But it was with the Second Battle of Weldon Railroad in August 1864, that Doctor Singletary witnessed the true horror of this war. The Richmond-Petersburg campaign encompassed a number of battles around Petersburg in its effort to protect Richmond, Capitol of the Confederacy. At a place called Globe Tavern, the Union troops once more tried to disrupt the Weldon-Wilmington Railroad that provided the lifeline for Petersburg and Richmond. This time, Lt. Gen. Ulysses Grant ordered Brig. Gen. Griffin to completely destroy the track. So on August 20, 1864, after fierce fighting and many casualties the Confederates pulled back from Globe Tavern. Consequently, they lost the Weldon-Wilmington Railroad. Thereafter they were forced to cart supplies to Petersburg by mule and wagon.

On August 25, 1864, Dr. Singletary walked into the Garysburg Confederacy Hospital and gawked at the bedlam he found inside. No longer were the sheets crisp and clean. No longer were the floors scrubbed and spotless. No longer were the cloth-covered worktables organized and unsoiled. Soldiers screamed, moaned, and reached pitiful, bloody hands out to whomever they felt could help them. Sheets were soaked with blood and mud. Dirty dressings were scattered about on the floor where they were hastily tossed. The bloody instruments on the worktable were continuously in use with no effort being made to clean them before the doctor moved on to another patient.

The once smiling, cheerful women who attended the patients looked harried and weary. Their clothes were bloodstained and tears streamed down their cheeks. In the corner of the room, Dr. Singletary became aware of an obscure pile of debris. He focused on the pile of rubbish in the corner, walked slowly across the room, and leaned forward to examine it. He recoiled in horror when he realized he was looking at a stack of human limbs. Feet, hands, legs, arms…just tossed aside as if they were dinner scraps being collected for hungry hunting dogs.

"Doctor, Doctor," a frantic voice yelled across the room. "Please help me here."

Doctor Singletary recognized Mrs. Harris, the chubby, smiling, tireless Garysburg lady who had always been there rendering help. Today, however, her entire demeanor had changed. There was a look of panic as she struggled to restrain a very young man who was scrambling out of the bed. His arm appeared to be hanging by a mere scrap of skin, and he was bleeding profusely. Doctor Singletary hurried across the room.

"Here, son, I'm a doctor. Let me help you." He wrapped his arms around the torso of the soldier and gently laid him down.

"Why he's just a boy," Dr. Singletary thought. "He's no older than Willis."

"Doctor," gasped the boy, "Don't let them take my arm. Please don't let them cut off my arm." And the boy soldier looked in horror at the pile of limbs in the corner of the room. Blood spurted from his wound every time the soldier spoke or moved.

"Mrs. Harris, help me here," said Doctor Singletary as he struggled to tear the shirt off the patient in order to apply a tourniquet. Suddenly he realized the soldier was no longer resisting. He was limp and his eyes stared unblinkingly at the doctor. Doctor Singletary backed away as he realized that the boy soldier was dead.

Mr. Harris burst into tears. "Another one," she wept. "Yet another one." And she fled from the room.

Doctor Singletary could not believe the state of the hospital. It had gone from a clean efficient facility to one of utter chaos and despair. He was shaken back to reality by the approach of another doctor.

"What happened here?" asked Doctor Singletary

in disbelief.

"General Grant has done his mischief up at Globe Tavern. They whipped our boys," replied the other doctor. "After a four-day battle we've lost control of the railroad and took a thrashing to boot. Why, these soldiers are no more than boys."

"I know," said Doctor Singletary, a look of distress on his face. "And my boy, Willis, is up there…up fighting at the Petersburg Siege."

"Do you know exactly where?"

"No," said Doctor Singletary.

The weary doctor rubbed his red-veined eyes and said, "Well, I pray he is safe, Doctor, but at this moment we have other fathers' sons to attend."

"Yes," whispered Doctor Singletary, "other fathers' sons."

During the week, Doctor Singletary moved from

one badly wounded soldier to another. Sleep deprivation and the trauma of being immersed in human tragedy soon took its toll, and the stunned doctor moved wordlessly from one soldier to another. He treated abdominal wounds, head wounds, broken bones, and did three amputations. Doctor Singletary would not, however, amputate a limb without the consent of the patient. He always explained the likelihood of gangrene and the possibility of an agonizing death, but ultimately he left the decision to amputate up to the soldier. The earlier image of the young soldier and how he beseeched him not to take his arm was still fixed in his mind. It was these ghastly recollections that Doctor Singletary brought home with him day after day.

Chapter 15

It was an unbearable time for Dr. Singletary. Abel watched as his good doctor aged. He grew thin...almost emaciated. Dr. Singletary reacted nervously to every sound, especially night sounds. He waited anxiously for the footsteps of a messenger bringing news about the battles and most particularly about Willis. Sleep was impossible, and many times Abel passed the doctor's room to hear his voice ever so low whispering to the portrait of his lovely Angela.

Dr. Singletary waited daily for news from the Petersburg Siege, and when it came, it was not good. As reparation, the good doctor spent many hours at Confederate Hospital, always hoping that someone would care for Willis in kind...if, God forbid, such a need arose.

Millie, Lori, and Willa were very mindful of their

father's stressful life. Millie took over most of the doctor's office practice and even made house calls during the day. If it was necessary to make house calls at night, Abel would drive her. Lori and Willa took care of the house.

The runaway hidden in his home was also worrisome. As the war raged on, conductors found travel more and more treacherous. Also, the man's recovery had not come quickly and the chances of his being discovered grew daily. To complicate matters, Tiny took a fancy to the handsome, young run-away. They learned he was called Obadiah, and Tiny announced to Bella that she would go with Obadiah when he made his dash for freedom. Bella reminded Tiny that she did not need to run away to find freedom for Dr. Singletary had already given her freedom. To this, Tiny simply declared she loved Obadiah. So, one morning Dr. Singletary was awakened by a terrifying wail. It was Bella, who upon awakening could find no trace of Tiny or Obadiah. Gone, also, were Tiny's papers confirming that she was a free Negro.

Adding to Dr. Singletary's concern was his beloved Willa. Unknown to Willa, Dr. Singletary learned of her affair with the mad minister's son. He feared that Willa might make the same reckless decision as Tiny if he interfered in their love affair. He could not bear the thought of losing Willa; so, although apprehensive about their affair, he chose to be watchful, silent, and patient.

Constant anxiety at home was another reason Dr. Singletary spent more and more time at Garysburg Confederate Hospital. Many times he would stay several days or even a week. When he could no longer endure to watch the pain, agony, and inhumanity suffered by the wounded soldiers, he'd go home. There he found little respite from worry, for he was forced to witness beautiful Willa's deception with the minister's son and Bella's grief in the loss of Tiny. Then, when the pain at home became insufferable, he would again return to the Hospital. And so it went.

One cold night, Abel was awakened by the sound of horse's hoofs. He leapt out of bed and looked out onto the back yard. Limbs of the leafless pecan trees were silhouetted against a large, orange, autumnal moon. The horse pulling the doctor's black barouche trotted wearily into view. Instead of stopping beside the back door, it continued directly to the barn. Abel dashed out of his cabin and ran frantically to the barn.

"Whoa, horse," he called over and over. But the horse did not stop until it entered the barn. When he entered Abel found the horse standing inside the barn hungrily eating oats from a hanging bucket.

"Where be da doctor?" said Abel more to himself than the horse. He rushed to the wagon and looked inside. There on the floor below the driver's seat lay the crumpled body of Dr. Singletary.

Abel wailed and gently lifted the doctor from the wagon. He wept and cradled the body as he would a child. Staggering, he carried him across the yard. Bella rushed from their cabin. When she saw who her husband carried, she fell to her knees and raised her arms heavenward.

"Oh, sweet Jesus, no," she screamed, "no!"

Abel looked up at the orange moon with its golden aura. Tears streamed down his face. He sobbed, "Oh God, he jest be wore out. His big ole' heart jest plum wore out."

& & &

No one dared hope that Willis might attend his father's funeral or that he would even learn of his death. Nonetheless, he arrived the day of the funeral dressed in ragged gray his sunken eyes brimming with tears. He lamented that through his death, his father brought him home. That Willis had traveled through the war-torn countryside and reached Seaboard alive was in itself a miracle.

"It was meant to be," said Lori. "God meant for Willis to get home safely."

At the cemetery service, Willa sat beside her twin

and held his hand affectionately. They sat around the beautiful grave house Mr. Davis had built for Charles and Angela Singletary. The house was a wooden construction painted white. It had a gable roof, two glass windows, and bright green shutters. There was gingerbread trim along the roofline and it was enclosed by a white picket fence. It was just large enough to contain two graves, two gravestones, and two headstones.

As the ceremony dragged on, Willa's cloak that-had been so carefully wrapped about her-fell away.

"Did he know?" Willis whispered. "Did papa know?" And he looked squarely at her slightly swollen belly.

Willa's blue eyes filled with tears. "I did not have the heart to tell him for I knew how disappointed he would be. But I think he guessed."

"Does he know?" asked Willis nodding slightly in the direction of the minister's son.

"No," said Willa. "His father has been called to another charge, and he will accompany him. I don't want to cause any complications."

"It's alright," said Willis patting her hand comfortingly. "We shall take care of you."

Chapter 16

Millie and Lori did not acknowledge Willa's pregnancy until early February.

"Willa," said Millie in a matter of fact manner, "we must soon prepare for the birth of your child."

"Shall we call a doctor?" asked Lori.

"No," Millie snapped. "The last time we asked for another doctor's help, mama died. No, we shall deliver our baby ourselves."

Lori nodded in wholehearted agreement.

The kind citizens of Seaboard were aware of Willa's delicate condition. Although curiosity ran high, they gathered ranks around the young woman and vigorously defended her against any mean-spirited gossip. Dr. Singletary had been much revered in this community, and protecting his young daughter was seen as a community mission.

March 1865, arrived. Forsythia bloomed beside the roadways and tiny green points pushed their ways through the rich black earth. Birds chirped and claimed their nesting places in bushes and trees where miniature leaves unfurled like pieces of sheer, delicate paper. With the splendor of nature's awakening came the alarming news that Petersburg had fallen on March 25. The people of Northampton County scrambled for news about their sons and husbands who fought in the siege. Millie, Lori, and Willa sat on the front porch listening intently for approaching hoof beats of couriers' horses as they brought news from the front. Even before the exhausted dispatch rider dismounted, he was besieged by families pleading for any information that might give them hope that their loved ones were still alive. The wait was excruciating.

On March 31, 1865, a hush settled on the house on Main Street. Outside a gentle spring rain fell. A squirrel sat on the front porch rail, his tail lifted over his head in umbrella fashion, and a one-eyed cat eyed a robin that bathed meticulously in a large mud puddle. In contrast, inside the house there was great excitement. Willa's time had arrived. Millie immediately took control of the birthing while Lori and Bella assisted and spoke to Willa in encouraging and loving tones. Willa continuously called for her soul mate...her twin, Willis. She swore that if the child were a boy he would be called Willis. Just as the sun set, the rooster crowed three times.

"That ain't a good sign," whispered Bella to Lori. Millie cut her a cautionary glance.

Just as it seemed that Willa could no longer help, there came a robust, impatient cry. Willa herself began to cry...not so much from joy as from exhaustion.

"Your baby is here, Willa," said Millie reaching down to lift the screaming baby. She wiped the baby's face, swaddled it, and handed it to Lori.

Willa sobbed, "Is it a boy?"

189

"Yes, sweet thing," said Bella patting Willa's hand. "It be a little boy."

As Bella and Lori took care of the baby, Millie looked after her patient. Willa cried softly. No one spoke.

Finally Willa stretched out her arms and said, "Let me have him."

Bella handed her the child, and Willa cuddled him close to her. The baby turned his tiny head and began searching for her breast.

"What shall we name him? I have only considered Willis," Willa said.

Lori answered eagerly, "Willis, of course. We should call him Willis Too...T-O-O."

"Willis Too?" repeated Willa.

Lori said, "Yes, Willis Too because he has a loud scream just like our other Willis. Willis Too is certainly suitable."

Millie, Bella, and Willa looked doubtful. Then suddenly they all began to laugh.

"Then Willis Too it shall be," said Millie, bending over to kiss her young sister and then their baby.

Abel made sure that the news spread throughout the town. Bells rang, not only for Willis Too but to honor his beloved grandfather, Dr. Charles Singletary.

& & &

All too soon mellow spring days gave way to the hot days of summer for which eastern North Carolina is famous. Willa adored her precious son. She would hold Willis Too, sit on the porch, and watch the soldiers pass on their long march back to their homes. They looked little more than skeletons and wore gray rags that were barely identifiable as uniforms. Many were wounded, and they were always hungry. Millie doctored the wounded as best she could and wished aloud that her father were there.

"But he is here, Millie," Lori would say softly. "We could never do this without Papa."

Lori and Bella fed the starving men with food from their own meager stores. They all hoped aloud that if Willis were walking home, someone would show him the same kindness. But most comforting to the soldiers was Willis Too. Willa walked him among the weary men and allowed them to hold him and play with him. He would bounce and coo and reach for their noses and ears. Willa watched tears roll down the men's cheeks as they thought of babies they had left behind an eternity ago.

Willa repeatedly asked about Willis Singletary. Once a one-legged soldier reported that he thought he shared a trench with a man named Willis but did not know his last name. Day after day Willa waited and rushed to meet every group of soldiers who came into sight. And day after day she was disillusioned as the faces of strangers passed.

It was one of those hot evenings in 1865 just before June turned into July. Willa lay in bed unable to sleep. She listened to the night sounds…a dog barking in the distance, crickets in the grass, and an owl calling in the distance. She studied patterns on the walls created by moonlight shining through the lace curtains. She watched as an eastern breeze blew gently and turned the curtains into billowing white clouds. Willis Too cooed and gurgled happily. The stillness was peaceful, reassuring. How she wished that Willis were here. She had so much to tell him…so much to share about Willis Too's father and how lonely it was since Tiny ran away. She longed for her twin…her soulmate.

Suddenly the gentle breeze became more intense. At first the curtains blew more forcefully, but then they began to snap wildly taking on disquieting shapes. Wilis Too began to gurgle nosily and flay his chubby legs and arms about excitedly. Willa suddenly felt cold. She jumped out of bed, ran across the room, and slammed down the window. She rushed to Willis Too's cradle and stared down at her precious baby. Willis Too smiled and chortled as he gazed into empty space above his crib...a void that a rather tall person would fill.

Willa did not know how long she stood beside Willis Too's cradle. She watched as the child thrashed about excitedly, laughing, and smiling into the emptiness. Abruptly, the wind subsided and the house became eerily still. Willis Too began to fret and looked at his mother for comfort. Willa picked up her baby and cuddled him lovingly. Then she quietly left the room, walked across the hall, and opened the door to Willis' room. How strange it felt to come here and not find her twin. She sat on his bed and gently rocked Willis Too. Finally the baby's eyes closed, and Willa began to cry softly. Lori appeared in the door and rushed across the room to her sister.

"Willa, what's the matter?" she cried and took her in her arms.

Willa lifted her tear-stained face and sobbed, "Oh, Lori, Willis is gone. He died in a hospital in Richmond. Our brother is dead."

Alarmed by their voices, Millie rushed in. "What's wrong? Is Willis Too ill?"

Lori looked at her sister and sobbed, "Willis is dead, Millie. Willa said so."

Chapter 17

Although the women had not received an official death notice, it was accepted that Willis was indeed dead simply because 'Willa said so'. Lori and Millie knew the twins shared a mystical bond since birth. Their relationship was spiritual, extrasensory. So when Willa announced that Willis was dead, it was not questioned, and the family immediately began to prepare for his funeral and burial. Word spread quickly throughout Seaboard that Willa alleged Willis' death. Although there were skeptics who shook their heads in disbelief, there were others who recalled the many times Willa's predictions were accurate.

Every evening the women sat on the front porch awaiting the appearance of the black horse-drawn wagon bearing a wooden coffin. Abel and Bella sat on the steps, and occasionally Abel rose, walked to the end of the path, and looked intently up and down the road.

One evening he stood at his watch longer than usual. Then slowly he turned, walked back to the porch, and said solemnly, "Here he be a'comin' now."

The women rose and slowly walked to the road. In the distance, they saw the head of a restless black horse bobbing up and down. They began to walk toward the wagon.

"I'm looking for the family of Willis Singletary" the tired old driver said.

"We are his family," said Millie. "We've come to meet our brother."

Abel and the old man gently lifted the wooden coffin off the wagon, carried it to the house, and set it in the parlor in the same place Dr. Singletary had laid. Following Willa's premonition, they had begun to bring in fresh flowers every morning and place chairs for the viewing. Abel and the driver placed Willis on the large table that awaited his coffin. Then Abel slowly raised the coffin lid, and they all burst into tears. Willis looked so alive, that one almost expected him to rise up and embrace his sisters.

& & &

For three days Willis lay in the wooden coffin in the parlor of his home on Main Street. The morticians used much arsenic to preserve Willis' body for his long trip from Richmond. As the body of the young soldier was viewed, townspeople whispered that he looked so alive they expected him to jump up and declare that he was only playing one of his childish pranks.

One night after the visitors left, the family sat silently in the parlor saying their private goodbye to Willis, for tomorrow he would be buried.

Willa stood and walked to the coffin, looked down at Willis, and vowed, "My dear brother, you will have the loveliest of graves….and it will be safe. Safe, my dear brother, and you will never hurt again. I promise you will lay forever in peace beside Mama and Papa and someday…yes someday…we'll all be together."

Present Day

Chapter 18

The white SUV pulled onto the shoulder of the road beside a historical marker. The side door rolled open and a little girl bounced out. She looked to be about six or seven years old and was missing a front tooth. Her skin was light brown and she wore corn braids tied off with brightly colored beads. Her shorts were red and pink plaid and she wore red flip-flops which slapped noisily as she ran to the marker.

"Mama, mama," she squealed, "This is it. See, it says, *Singletary Family Cemetery.*"

The woman who got out of the SUV was smartly dressed. She was tall, slim, and light tan. "You're right, Millie, I believe we've finally found it." And she quickly moved to the marker and began to read.

The driver of the SUV was a tall, dark-skin man. He slowly got out of the SUV, joined her, and placed his arm around her shoulder. "I've never driven down so many dusty, rutty roads in all my life. I just hope it hasn't damaged the suspension on the SUV."

The woman gave him an annoyed look. "Which

is more important, Darren, your SUV or my finally finding the grave of my sixth-generation grandparents?"

The man hugged her shoulder and said, "Sorry hon. Just saying. I hope you find what you're looking for here. You don't know if they are actually buried here...." But he stopped as the woman and child rushed toward the gate to the cemetery.

There was a crunching sound from inside the van. "Come on out here, Josh," said the big man half-heartedly. "Show a little interest. This trip's not about you, it's for your mother. So look alert, get out of the van, and help her search for her long-lost dead family in yet another country cemetery."

A young man slowly skulked to the van door. He was a typical resentful fourteen-year-old who would rather be anywhere than with his family on a road trip searching cemeteries for hundred year old family graves. His baggy jeans were worn so low that any sudden movement might cause them to drop to the ground and a huge sweatshirt almost reached his knees. He stared with disgust at the countryside around him. His father motioned him to fall in as he moved toward the gate.

Once inside the gate, the little girl raced excitedly from one grave to another reading aloud the names, dates, and epitaphs. Her mother followed behind.

"Look Mama," the child screeched. There's no name on these…just CSA and a date."

"Maybe I can explain that to you," said a hoarse voice from the back of the cemetery. The child and mother started and turned to see an old man limping toward them. He was dressed in bib overalls and carrying a rake. He reached the woman just as her husband moved toward her. He took off his hat revealing on oily sweatband and said, "My name is Sam Davis the volunteer caretaker here at the Singletary Family Cemetery. I take care of this cemetery for the town of Seaboard." He nodded toward the license plate on the van and added, "Saw you are from out-of-state and thought you might need some help."

"Thank you," said the lady. "I am…"

But she was interrupted by the excited little girl. "You forgot to put names on some of your graves. How do you know who's buried there?"

The old man chuckled. "Now's that's a good observation and a good question. Walk over here with me." And he walked to the opposite side of the cemetery where he pointed to several rows of graves on which there were no names. "You see, young lady," he said. "After the big war, the Confederate soldiers started walking home and many of them didn't make it. They just dropped dead beside the road. Lots of them didn't have identification on them, so the Singletary family picked them up, brought them here, and buried them right in their own family cemetery."

The girl studied several graves carefully and said, "But all these stones have CSA carved on them. Who is CSA?"

"Why, CSA is not a person, it stands for Confederate States of America. That's who these young men fought for, and that's the only identification they had…that and the date they were buried."

Surprisingly the sullen young man asked, "Are there any more cemeteries around like this? I mean did other families bury unknown soldiers in their personal cemetery?"

The old man scratched his head. "Well, I can't say for sure, son, but I'd guess there are family cemeteries like this scattered all about North Carolina. You see, North Carolina was the last Southern state to join the Confederacy, yet they lost more troops than any other Confederate state. So it's not a stretch to think that many of those young soldiers died on their long march back to their homes in Carolina. Yes, I'd say more families than the Singletary family showed those unknown soldiers this same respect and reverence." And he waved his hand over the graves.

The woman said, "Thank you. That is quite interesting. I never thought about what happened to soldiers who died on their march back home. The Singletary family must have been a very kind family. I've heard so much about them all my life. You see, my seventh generation grandparents were Bella and Abel Singletary. They were slaves bought by Dr. Charles Singletary at a slave auction in Fayetteville, North Carolina, but within a few days Dr. Singletary gave them their freedom. They took his name and chose to stay on as his servants. To this day, my family holds

Dr. Singletary and his entire family in the highest regard. It is Abel and Bella Singletary's graves that I am looking for. I reasoned if I found the Singletary family cemetery I might find a clue as to where they are buried."

The old keeper beamed. "Well, my dear lady, you have happened upon the right place. Come on over here." And he turned and virtually hopped across the cemetery in the opposite direction.

In the distance was a small white building with a picket fence around it. The little girl sprinted ahead. "Look Mama, there's a play house right here in the middle of a cemetery. Hurry, let's go look at it."

The others hurried to keep up with the energetic girl. When they reached the small building, they were amazed at all the detail that went into the building. The house and picket fence both appeared to have been painted recently. There were four glass windows in the front and a paneled door with a polished brass door handle. Flowers bloomed in containers on the tiny porch and a small patch of grass stretched between the porch and fence.

"Fancy place to store your tools," said the father. The caretaker just grinned.

"Mama, I've never seen such a pretty playhouse in all my life," the girl exclaimed.

"Just wait till you see what is inside," the keeper said and he unlatched the gate, stepped on the porch, and turned the door handle. The girl pushed forward, scrambled into the building, and then there was total silence.

Her mother looked concerned. "You alright, honey?" Still silence.

The boy shoved his way onto the porch and into the house. *"Holy...."*

"Watch your mouth, boy," his father yelled and he and his wife entered the house.

Much to their amazement they found they were standing beside two tombstones complete with headstones. The woman moved forward and bent to read the engraving.

"Angela Singletary," she read. Then she moved to the next headstone, bent forward, and read, "Dr. Charles Singletary. This is them, Darren. This is

Angela and Charles. I've found their graves. Now if I could only..."

Finally the family backed out of the little house. The caretaker said, "You see this isn't a tool shed or a play house. This is what they called a grave house. *My* ancestor built this grave house for Angela Singletary, and he was instructed to build it large enough for Dr. Singletary to be buried alongside her. Grave houses were a tradition brought here by early settlers from other countries. In Europe they were intended to discourage grave robbers. You see bodies were often dug up and sold to medical schools. Also, in the past, people were often buried wearing fine jewelry. Well, that was just too much temptation for thieves. They'd just dig up the grave, and steal the jewelry and fill it right back in. Here in America, grave houses were thought to prevent wild animals from digging up the grave. Now I can't say that grave houses prevented any of these crimes from occurring, but it made those left behind feel like they'd done their best to protect their dearly departed.

"The more important a person, the more elaborate

their grave house. As you can see, the Singletary family was very highly thought of. It's the finest in the county and has been scrupulously maintained. That's how we got that historical marker. It's not so much to honor the Singletary family as to preserve a burial method no longer practiced. These four graves on the right are the graves of Dr. Singletary's four children. You might want to take a look at those too. But you were asking about Abel and Bella Singletary. If you'll just step over here," the keeper said as he walked to the left of the grave house.

There in the shade of an ancient oak tree were two gravestones crowned by headstones. Atop each headstone stood small statues of angels' wings spread wide and faces lifted heavenward. The young woman dropped to her knees, covered her face, and began to cry.

"Bella, Abel, I am your seventh-generation granddaughter. I have so much to tell you about Tiny and Obadiah," she sobbed.

Darren gathered his children close and whispered, "Come on, kids. Give your mama some time alone with

Bella and Abel. She's looked for them a long time. Let's see what else we can find."

The children laughed and played and raced through the cemetery playing tag, hide and seek, and reading the old epitaphs. The old caretaker said, "You know I'm always amazed how children love to play in a cemetery. Grown-ups find cemeteries spooky and off-putting, but kids…well, they seem to find some kind of peace here."

Sometime later the young woman joined them. Her eyes were red from crying but she had a smile on her face and a look of serenity. She and her family thanked the old cemetery caretaker for his time and for keeping the graves so well maintained.

"Now that you know where to find Bella and Abel, y'all come back to see them…anytime. We don't lock things up 'round here," the old man said.

The family began to climb into the SUV and the old man called out. "By the way, madam," he said, "I don't think I ever got your name."

She turned to him, smiled, and said, "My name is Wilhelmena. Wilhelmena Singletary. Just call me

Willa." And she smiled and waved as they drove down the dusty, rutty road.

From the Author

Writing historical fiction can be an especially challenging effort that requires the author to provide some distinction between fact and fiction. To that end I offer these brief explanations.

It is true that the Underground Railroad existed throughout slave holding states even into the war years. They were routes leading from the South into free Northern States. The runaway slaves were led by conductors who knew these routes well. As they fled they sought refuge in safe houses along the way. Symbols such as carvings, paintings and drawings were used to identify these safe houses. Shelter was provided along this treacherous trek by ministers, Quakers, and others who opposed slavery.

In reality the passing of a railroad through small southern villages caused much excitement and many changes in a community. In Concord, Northampton County, North Carolina, citizens were so awestruck by this modern machine that they changed the name of their village from Concord to Seaboard in honor of and appreciation to the railroad company, Seaboard Railroad.

In fact the railroads that crisscrossed Northampton County and, in particular, the Weldon railroads played crucial roles in transporting supplies and arms to the Confederate Army of Northern Virginia. One such crucial link in Northampton County was realized and resulted in Union General S. P. Spear and 5000 of his troops being dispatched in July 1863 to invade Northampton County. Their mission was to destroy the railway bridge over the Roanoke River in order to interrupt the supply line at Weldon. General Spear's mission failed when Confederate General Matt Ransom and his Confederate soldiers attacked and defeated Spears at Boone's Mill, just outside Seaboard, driving him back to Winton, North Carolina; and the railroad bridge survived.

Importantly, the railroads that ran through Weldon, North Carolina took arms and supplies from Wilmington to the Confederate troops under siege at Petersburg. This route did not go unnoticed by Union

General Ulysses S. Grant. He launched a campaign to destroy the Weldon lines into Virginia. The first Battle of Weldon Railroad was at a place called Jerusalem Plank in June, 1864. The battle was strategically called a draw. Then in August, 1864 the Second Battle of Weldon Railroad took place at Globe Tavern. Here the Union Army succeeded in retaking all the lost ground of the first Battle of Weldon Railroad and established a defensive position around Globe Tavern. The Union army gained its first decisive victory during the Siege of Petersburg.

Plainly, the horrendous battles that took place during this war required the most determined and dedicated doctors on both sides. Hospitals such as the Confederate Hospital housed in the Garysburg Methodist Church sprang up all over the country. Conditions described in this story are clearly documented.

At this point I departed from fact and drew upon my mind's eye. All the members of the Singletary family and citizens of Seaboard are the product of my imagination. Any similarities to these citizens living or dead are most certainly coincidental.

Sources

1. *Footprints in Northampton*, Northampton Country Bicentennial Committee, 1976.

2. Deering J. Roberts, M.D., Surgeon, Confederate States Army, *Field and Temporary Hospitals.*

3. Brandy Centolanza, *Surgical Practice in the Colonies*, Health Journal, February 2009.

4. Historic Weldon, North Carolina Railroad History, *The First Railroad Hub of the South,*
    http://www.historicweldonnc.com/history/railroad.

5. Graham Ford, *Phlebotomy: The Ancient Art of Bloodletting http://www.museumofquackery.com.*

6. John L. Konefes and Michael K. McGee, *Old Cemeteries, Arsenic, and Health Safety.*

215

7. *Selected Milestones in Cumberland County History 1754-2004, The Market House,* Cumberland County, North Carolina Public Library Information Center.

8. *"A Free and Independent State": North Carolina Secedes from the Union,* http://docsouth.unc.edu/highlights/secession , The University Library, The University of North Carolina, Chapel Hill, 2015.

9. African American Registry, *West Virginia Created by Secession From Southern Confederate State.* Referenced *The Encyclopedia Britannica*, Fifteenth edition, 1996.

10. Chris Calkins, Chief of Interpretation, Petersburg National Battlefield, *The Battle of the Weldon Road,* Blue & Gray Magazine, Vol. XXIII #5.

11. *Barouche,* http://en.wikipedia.org/wiki/Barouche.

12. *Prince Hall Freemasons and the Underground Railroad.* http://vimeo.com.

Made in the USA
Charleston, SC
26 May 2015